From Avinger to
Iroquois Street

Also by Carole L. Piller

From Avinger to Iroquois Street

Carole L. Piller

iUniverse, Inc.
New York Lincoln Shanghai

From Avinger to Iroquois Street

Copyright © 2006 by Carole L. Piller

iUniverse books may be ordered through booksellers or by contacting:

iUniverse
2021 Pine Lake Road, Suite 100
Lincoln, NE 68512
www.iuniverse.com
1-800-Authors (1-800-288-4677)

ISBN-13: 978-0-595-39154-7 (pbk)
ISBN-13: 978-0-595-83540-9 (ebk)
ISBN-10: 0-595-39154-0 (pbk)
ISBN-10: 0-595-83540-6 (ebk)

Printed in the United States of America

This novel is written with my parents in mind. My father left the small farming town of Avinger years ago venturing out to make his mark on the world. He met and wed my mother and I became their first born child. For that, I express my love and appreciation.

Acknowledgement

I would like to thank Simon, my husband and best friend, for his genuine encouragement. Without him, my life would have been one of boredom. I appreciate his enthusiasm and patience with all of my projects. I am grateful for his wisdom and ability to understand that the creativity in me must prevail.

1

Making a slight curve, an old olive pickup truck traveled on the highway toward the sun at a steady pace. Passing desolate fields with occasional tumbleweeds rolling by, the engine purred as it made its way. The truck's owner took pride in keeping the engine finely tuned, making it sound as if it were new. Billowy clouds moved slowly in the pale sky as a young couple drove in the blazing Arizona sun.

The back of the truck bulged from carrying all of their worldly possessions. In a corner closest to the truck's cab laid an old, hand-carved, wooden chest from the young woman's grandmother filled with linen, dishes, silverware, and a set of crystal glasses. Underneath the weathered tan tarpaulin were bags of clothing, cartons containing tools, a uniquely crafted bed frame made by the young man's grandfather, and a mattress stuffed with duck feathers. There were gifts they obtained from their wedding, new cookware, and other things they accumulated over the years.

Dennis and Louise were childhood sweethearts, married just months ago, now destined for Los Angeles to seek a new life for themselves. A former classmate lived there and informed the young man that whenever he was ready, to come and check it out. After several months of consideration, Dennis finally wrote his friend informing him that he would be there by the middle of the week.

)0(

Dennis' father was a carpenter by profession, whose father taught him. All of the sons, from the time they were strong enough to hold a hammer in their hand, assisted their father in his trade. The family was considered master carpenters for their expertise and stylistic approach. Dennis, the third oldest son, went to school as everyone did in Cass County, from first through twelfth grade. Their township of Avinger, Texas had a population of 600 people. If you were not related, you darn sure knew everyone and all of their business. Young people could hardly wait to leave town after graduating from high school, casting aside their stodgy past for bigger and better things.

Life in town was typical of every small country town, with its inhabitants ranging from the well to do with money and prosperous land, to the impoverished dirt farmer. The general run-of-the-mill jobs available were farming, raising livestock, picking cotton, and either working at the grain or saw mills. Although the closest oil refinery was within thirty miles and the pay was excellent, jobs were not readily available because people never left, unless they retired or died.

To receive the services of a doctor, hospital, or pharmacy, they traveled twenty miles to the nearest towns, to either Jefferson to the south or Hughes Spring to the north. There were several midwives and two nurses, one black and one white, whose skills were well utilized, especially in emergencies. Depending on the nature of the services provided, acceptable payment arrangements were made among the parties. Payment could be made in the form of hens, eggs, vegetables, and livestock or building and repair work. The doctors were paid the same way. It was not unusual to have a bill from the doctor's office for fifteen dollars, partial payment of ten dollars cash, and the balance paid in goods or services. In the parking lot of the doctor's office, it was quite common to see a truck filled with fresh produce and livestock, waiting to be bartered off. The position of a physician in small towns did not mean that he or she was wealthy in the monetary sense, but wealthy in the abundance of acquired things.

With not much of anything to do in town, there were two restaurants for dining. The local diner seated and served whites, but blacks could place takeout orders from the backdoor. The other restaurant was a pizza parlor, which doubled as an ice cream parlor. Tables in the pizza parlor were covered with the popular starched red and white gingham tablecloths. This restaurant was more progressive and allowed all of its customers to be seated within it. The front section with the window view was for the whites and the back half was for the blacks.

The general store smelled of a conglomeration of new leather, tobacco, sweet candy, toiletries, and dried goods. Lighting was dim because the owner never bothered to install modern lights. The lights were a crude form of electricity that resembled the remnants of old gas lanterns, barely providing enough light to see the merchandise in the store. The owner sold everything from groceries to farm and ranch equipment to firearms. Even though the grocery store was more modern and brightly lit, it had trouble competing with the general store because it did not allow customers to buy on credit.

There were two barbershops. The one for whites was situated in the center of town with the traditional red and white candy stripe light post outside the shop. Horace Brown ran the black barbershop business out of a shack off of Rural Route 1. Two black sisters ran the hair salons. Pearl and Hattie were wise enough to attend beauty school to learn how to do both black and white hair. Each hired their daughters to assist them with shampooing and scheduling appointments. Their businesses were so lucrative that they never lacked customers, especially with the heat from the hot Texas sun burning down on their heads to sweat out a new hairdo.

In the summer, it was hot enough to simmer bacon on a rooftop. Outside, there was no relief from the heat. Folks adapted to the temperature by wearing lightweight clothing with a bandana around the neck or on the head, which helped capture perspiration, or by wearing a hat or using an umbrella. The sun's sizzling touch beat down on their bodies, making it feel as if they suddenly gained fifty pounds, which was profusely sweated off by the end of the day. Using a hand fan proved futile because it only brought a few nanoseconds of cooler air. The effort generated more heat, but yet, they continued to fan. Some kept a jug of water close by to quench their thirst. Others drank corn liquor or whiskey, but that is completely another story. With as much of an effect of a child's pinwheel, electric fans stirred up the air. If you did not situate yourself directly in front of them, it was as if they were not turned on. Air conditioners were expensive to buy but were a good investment, if you could afford one. They paid for themselves by working as hard as mules distributing cool air, warding off the heat.

The sun's rays served them well. Without it, the farmers could not grow their crops. The long dog days of summer exposed them to a dry climate without rain, causing droughts. When they could, the wise farmers and ranchers kept water reservoirs, ponds, and developed irrigation systems to retain the water they needed, but sometimes that just was not enough.

The air was so thick that it was too much work for a mosquito to sting you. They leisurely hung low during the day and waited to attack at nightfall. The flies, garbed with their insulated gear seemed to relish the heat. They encircled the livestock and waited for them to drop their excrement so that they could share a tasty feast. The poor horses and cattle shook them off and swung their tails in a rhythmic beat, shooing them away. The red ants stayed cool in their small mounds of anthills, of which there were many. They were the ones you had to stand guard against. Covertly swarming and undetectable, they crawled upon you, waited for the leader's cue, and then attacked in unison with ferocious bites that hurt bad enough to make you think you jumped into a pool of fire.

The winter season was a breeze to get through. The coldest it ever reached was about sixty degrees. Heavy winter coats were unheard of. Snow was something mystical that folks only heard or read about. Most lived their entire lives without ever seeing it, unless they ventured north.

There were four churches, a Catholic and Baptist church for the white folks, and a Baptist and Methodist church for the black folks. Black ministers were scarce in Avinger. They maintained two churches in different towns, therefore, every other Sunday a church held service without the presence of a minister.

Not many of the young people had an inclination to go to college. The few of them that did, could not afford it, and even if they decided to go, they would have to travel to Marshall, Texas over forty-five miles away. That was too far to walk. Some stayed home and took whatever jobs were available. Others were content to continue the legacy of farming and ranching as their ancestors had done by dealing with the vicious cycle of hard work and hard times, because this existence was all they knew. If they could not save to buy their own farms, they were content with living the life of a sharecropper. It took a daring soul to change this sequence, by taking the initiative to leave the town while young enough not to become complacent. The adventurous ones headed for some metropolis such as Los Angeles, San Francisco, Chicago, or New York to live and work, temporarily living with relatives or friends who had also escaped the small town life.

2

As an accomplished carpenter, Dennis saw himself hundreds of miles away from Avinger, Texas in a place where he could expand his knowledge by possibly working for a major construction company. Where he would go from there was unknown, but this would be a start. He and his brothers frequently accompanied their father throughout the state to work on an assortment of jobs they acquired by word of mouth.

Emulating his father's life was not enough to sustain him; discernibly, he wanted more. When he visited large cities such as Dallas, Fort Worth, and Houston, the different architectural structures, bright city lights, and activities stirred up overwhelming feelings within him, beckoning him to be a part of them. The unfamiliarity of the fast pace and the way that things never stayed the same caused his senses to want to burst with exhilaration. Ensnarled by the day-to-day humdrum life, he needed to escape from Avinger before becoming consumed. Envisioning a future of growth with Louise, Dennis knew it would not happen in their matchbox town.

Dennis was raised with his siblings, three brothers, and two sisters in a modern ranch styled home that started out as a tiny four-room house, built by his grandfather. His father converted it into a bi-level ranch with five bedrooms and a living room with a window the length of the room. The view from the window displayed multi-shades of green with patches of colors from the fields of the neighboring farmland and hillside. The family gathering place was the huge kitchen that housed two long tables and chairs proudly made by John and his sons, which accommodated all of them on Sunday during their family dinner.

John Clark towered over his wife, Mary, by a foot and a half. The females in the family reached average heights and the males were slightly taller. Each child's physical features were an amalgamation of both of their parents, similar, but with his or her own unique characteristics. Dennis, like his brothers, was strikingly handsome and kept his hair cut close. He was stocky with strong broad shoulders and muscular arms and legs, which were developed from the demands of carpentry and farm work. Because he loved working with his hands, it was hard for him to remain idle for long.

The Clark family, being that they were not diehard farmers, did not have acres upon acres of land. Their neighbors had forty acres or more to grow their crops, raise animals, and cut trees for lumber. The Clarks only owned twenty acres, which included a five-acre pond. This was just enough land for Mary Clark and her two daughters to maintain for growing grains, fruits, and vegetables for their family. They owned a small tractor which they used while working in the field, a couple of milking cows, two roosters, approximately three dozen hens, a few turkeys, and geese, including one mean ole gander. What farm would not be complete without dogs for hunting and cats to catch field mouse?

Whenever John Clark's carpentry business was sluggish, he and his sons assisted Mary and the girls in their field plowing, planting, fertilizing, weeding, and harvesting. One son who was two years younger than Dennis still lived at home. The two eldest sons were married and had four children between them. One of them lived in town and the other one lived on an acre of John Clark's land. The daughters were in school so they performed their chores prior to leaving home and completed them upon their return. Homework was always done in the evening after dinner. Since the town was a farming community, school started at ten in the morning and was over by two in the afternoon.

The Clarks were a clannish group, and if you did anything to cause conflict with one of them, you'd have to take on the lot of them. Mary, the ardent business minded person, taught her husband how to operate his carpentry business at a level that would be the most beneficial, without him losing too much profit. If one of his customers was dissatisfied with a portion of his work, Mary stepped in to show him how to collect for the work that was completed, and whenever possible dismantle any of the work that was questionable. She suggested that John urge his customer to find someone else to complete the job, and in most cases, no one could provide the same quality of work. She was also skilled in writing elegant threatening letters to an unpaid customer. You would have thought she was a lawyer. Her parents were Baptist missionaries who operated a church and a small school in Houston. Mary had been one of their prime students.

During her second year of college, she met John while he and his assistant were replacing the weathered pillars to the college's main building. Mary passed by him one day while he was standing on a ladder working. She commented, "Fine job you're doing up there." Smitten by her remark and her good looks, he found various tasks that needed to be performed in and around the school so that he could continue to be around her. He sold his services to the college's president and during this time, a courtship ensued between him and Mary that led to their desire to marry. After several whirlwind discussions with her parents about leaving school to move to another county to marry John, they married eight months after meeting. Mary started a family and never returned to school.

Initially, Mary's parents were skeptical of the marriage and rejected them. After seeing how well John could provide for their daughter, they endorsed their union, considering it a wise one.

Mary did not spend all of her time in the field; she also had cooking, canning, and cleaning to do. She assigned weekly chores for her husband and children. When the guys were out of town on jobs, she hired relatives and friends to help her. She formed a baking group and they sold their goods to the general store, the grocery store, both restaurants, and the two gas stations in town. With expansion of their territory, they delivered goods to neighboring towns and saw profits that were beneficial to the group. Mary maintained excellent bookkeeping records for the baking group, John's business, and the church. She was someone you definitely wanted to befriend. When Gilbert Cleveland broke his arm and could not operate his tractor for two months, Mary led a drive that got the people in town to take turns performing his farm chores. She had John construct a fruit and vegetable stand on the road by Gilbert's house and sold his produce along with her group's baked goods, showing Gilbert proceeds he had never dreamed of.

Even though Mary was the industrious one, John could not be taken for granted. Smart enough to realize not to be threatened by Mary's initiatives, he learned from them. Operating his carpentry business in a professional manner, he got more jobs than he needed and they were able to save money for rainy days. John was as authentic as a man could be. He helped raised his children to respect one another, encouraging their intelligence and productivity. The Clark family was well respected in their community. John wanted his daughters to go to college and be smart like their mother. Since each of his sons worked as his apprentice, he felt he provided them with enough knowledge for a financially sound existence.

Encountering a new technique or equipment, John would either find out about it himself, or send one of his sons to learn about it, and then teach the rest of them. If new equipment was required, they purchased it, even if it meant applying for credit at the bank.

Of course, John discussed matters like this with his wife, and her negotiating skills were a must with the loan officer. One day the loan officer became so frustrated with Mary's cankerousness that he suggested that she consider taking his job. Her response to him was for him to exchange seats with her, and within minutes she successfully negotiated a deal that was acceptable to everyone. John beamed that day, and the next time he went out of town on a job, he brought home a new stove for his wife. The love that Mary and John exhibited to their family gave their children the crucial ingredient of the way a family should exist.

3

When Dennis married, his parents allowed him to bring his wife into their home so they could save money. Louise made a perfect addition to the family and their acceptance of her was as if she was another daughter. One year younger than Dennis, when she was twelve years old, they developed a crush on each other. After their marriage, Dennis tried persuading Louise to relocate to a city where they could reside, so he could better utilize his carpentry skills. Louise knew that day was coming. With false hope, she prayed that Dennis would find enough contentment in their marriage that would make him want to remain in Avinger. Her roots were in Avinger, and this is where she wanted to stay. To her dismay, his desire to leave grew, and nothing she could do or say would deter him. Each foresaw their future in a different light, hoping the other would change their minds on their positions. When Louise realized she was fighting a losing battle, she surrendered. Promising to join him later, Louise suggested for him to go on without her and find suitable housing. Unequivocally refusing to leave her, Dennis was fearful of being in a new place without her, but if he had to, he would go. Louise's apprehensions led her to seek the advice of her mother. "Your place is with your husband. If he wants to go, you should accompany him," her mother advised. "If things don't work out, you can always come home."

)0(

Dennis heard that California was the place to prosper. It was the early 1950's, and businesses were flourishing. They packed their 1948 Ford pickup truck with all their belongings and set out for Los Angeles. Reluctant as she was, Louise enjoyed the time they spent traveling together. Other than the two-day honeymoon they spent in Houston, they never spent any time alone.

Riding with the windows down, Louise's hair flowed freely as they made their way in the searing sun. Her golden brown skin glistened, and her full lips accented her beautifully sculptured face. Dennis snuck side-glimpses at her, deliberating he was the luckiest man in the world. When they stopped for gas and needed to relieve themselves, they were directed to an outhouse in the field or were told that there was no washroom for *coloreds*. This did not bother Dennis because he was accustomed to this kind of treatment, when he traveled with his father. Louise, on the other hand was outdone and found the practice deplorably annoying. Dennis would pamper her and provide her with a jug filled with fresh water that he pumped or drew from a well or got from a hose so she could bathe herself. Once they went through all the food from their packed lunch, they sought out restaurants. Many of the restaurants along the way would not serve them, or they would have to go to the backdoor to order food.

"This is just like at home," commented Louise. "Will we ever escape this kind of treatment?"

"I don't know for sure Lou, but from what I've heard, Los Angeles will welcome us. We won't have to worry about this kind of thing anymore."

Taking turns driving until they both declared they were too tired to travel any further, at nightfall Dennis would pull off the road to find a field for them to make camp for the night. Those side-glances he had given her during their drive stirred in his groin, and when they stopped, he smothered Louise with his kisses and his body.

Because they lived in his parent's house, they were never free to express their love above a whisper. In the fields, Louise would let out the sweetest purrs. "I love you Dennis Clark. I love you so much. You make me feel so good," she would say. When she would make her announcement this gave him even more momentum to "drive her home." She hollered and squealed like a pig in heat. He knew when she was ready for him to make that final move that brought them to their special place. Afterward, Louise would lie in his arms and fall asleep. Dennis would wake her early before a passerby could discover them. He was "Johnny on the spot" with that jug of water for her to use for bathing. They took their time traveling to Los Angeles and enjoyed their nightly stops. By the time they reached California, the blatant racism that they had experienced lessened. They were able to use the restrooms in the gas stations and eat in restaurants. Louise accepted this with much satisfaction.

4

Once in Los Angeles, Dennis stopped to use a payphone to call his friend, but no one answered. Noticing a construction site across the street, he walked over to ask for employment. The construction boss informed him that he did not require any additional help, but he referred him to two other locations that might. With directions in hand, Dennis and Louise set out in search of them.

The next location was in a business district where an office building was under construction. Dennis was directed to the construction boss' office.

After knocking on the door a man said, "What in the hell do you want?"

Surprised by the harsh response he received, but not enough to be dissuaded, Dennis replied, "Excuse me sir for bothering you, but I'm seeking employment and a man outside here directed me to you." His cultivated southern drawl was prevalent in his speech. Dennis stepped back as the man opened the door for him to come in.

"Who sent you in here? Was it Ralph?" he asked with anger.

"You think I need help?" he replied with sarcasm. "I'm waiting for shipments that haven't come in. I don't have enough manpower to get the job done and I'm behind in my schedule. I don't need another lazy ass man standing around not working. I need a willing and able body that is interested in working and making money!"

"Well, I'm your man," said Dennis proudly. "I'm a carpenter by profession."

"I don't need a goddamn carpenter. Right now, I need a construction worker! Please stop wasting my time!"

Dennis smiled as he spoke, "Sir, I've worked on construction jobs for several years, and I can do almost anything."

"Oh yeah? Prove it," said the boss.

Perplexed by his statement Dennis asked, "What do you want me to do?"

Pointing to a box on the floor and issuing him a temporary hard hat, the boss said, "Take that goddamn box of rivets and bolts up to the supervisor on the sixth landing! Get him to sign this order and return it to me!"

"Is that all?"

"No, tell the idiot that sent you in here to get his ass in here quick!"

Grasping the heavy box of hardware, Dennis exited the office to find Ralph.

"Was the boss hard on you?" asked Ralph with a smirk on his face.

"Yep, but he didn't bother me."

"Sorry, about that man, but when things aren't going well he has a terrible disposition. Did he hire you?"

"No, not yet," replied Dennis, "he has given me an assignment. By the way, he wants to see you."

"Thanks," said Ralph heading for the office.

From the office window, the construction boss and Ralph watched Dennis skillfully catch the crane elevator to the sixth landing. The boss winked his eye with approval at Ralph. This was nothing new to Dennis because he had experienced this sort of thing while working with his father. Upon his return to the boss' office, he was hired on the spot. The construction boss introduced himself and told him he could start work the next morning at seven o'clock.

Ralph referred him to the group of *colored* workers on the fourth level of the steel structure for advice on a place to stay.

Observing the construction workers as they operated the large cranes and moved heavy steel beams was mesmerizing to Louise. The community of workers was fascinating to watch, as they worked in clusters, welding steel or drilling holes while fiery sparks flew from their equipment. When she saw her husband climb onto the crane elevator, both times she was horrified watching his elevations and descents in the open space. When he returned to her, he bore a wide toothed grin and handed her a piece of paper with addresses and directions on it.

"Well, what happened?" she asked impatiently.

"I got a job and two places for us to check out to see if we can stay there," he replied, quite delighted with himself.

"I thought we were going to stay with your friend, Henry for a while."

"Why stay there if we can find a place of our own?" he asked, especially with the fresh remembrance of the past few nights they spent together alone.

"Your luck is unbelievable! Let's go check out these places," she said as she grinned.

They read the instructions and drove off in the direction of the first address. It was on Pottawatomie Drive where several apartment buildings lined the street. People of color and Latinos traveled the street in cars and trucks. Two old ladies carrying bags of groceries were walking down the street while children ran past them almost knocking one of them down. The women cursed at the children for being so reckless. Garbage was haphazardly lying on the pavement. Momentarily, their attention was drawn to the middle of the block, where they observed two men in a heated argument, which resulted from a collision involving their vehicles. After finding the building with the correct address, they were disappointed because it was the worst looking building on the block. It had trash and broken glass on the stairs and broken windows on the first and third floors. Grimacing, they shook their heads and drove off in search of the next address.

The second address led them miles away, to a neighborhood where there were houses with spacious yards. The street had a peaceful serenity about it, birds were chirping and you could hear the humming of an occasional bee or two. They found the address on a yellow three-story house with whitewashed window frames and colorful flowers at the top of the stairs. In the truck, Louise neatly combed her hair and applied a little lipstick to her lips. Not without receiving opposition from Dennis, she insisted that he change his shirt and wash his face before exiting the truck.

Climbing to the top of the stairs, they knocked on the door. A short middle-aged black woman with slightly graying dark hair and neatly combed curls surrounding her face appeared. Through aged lines of distinction, she displayed a warm smile.

She said, "Can I help you young people?"

"Hello ma'am, we'd like to speak to Mrs. Caldwell about the furnished apartment she has for rent," said Dennis without stopping to take a breath, in his southern drawl. "My name is Dennis Clark and this here is my wife, Louise. We'd like to see the apartment, if it's still available."

"I'm sorry, but I rented it out to a gentleman and his son yesterday."

The young couple looked disheartened.

Louise asked, "Do you know where we can find a place to stay because we have been traveling for quite a while coming from Texas." The disparity could be heard in her voice.

"Sorry, I don't."

As they turned to descend upon the stairs, Dennis turned back toward her.

"Thanks ma'am," he said, as his hand touched the broken wooden railing. Thoughtfully, he added, "When we get settled, I'd like to come back here and repair this for you if you don't mind, ma'am."

"Are you a handyman? I need to have some work done around here, and the last *fella* I had, moved out of the neighborhood."

Smiling as he unconsciously expanded his chest, he announced, "I'm a carpenter by trade ma'am, and I'd be glad to help you once we get settled."

Raising her finger in the air, as a sudden thought occurred to her, she said, "There is an old house in the back that I've been using as a shed and is in need of repair. If you and your missus can fix it up you're welcome to stay in it. I'd charge you $15.00 a week to stay there, if you want it."

Dennis and Louise gestured a nonverbal nod, expressing their acceptance to her offer.

Dennis stated, "We'd be happy to take it."

"Not so fast!" Mrs. Caldwell tenaciously announced. "You haven't seen it yet. As I said it is in great need of work."

"We don't care," said Louise happily, "we aren't afraid of work."

"Okay, then let me get the key and show it to you."

While waiting for the older woman's return, they perused the street. The houses were moderately large and were two to three stories tall. Even though each house probably took up two to three city lots, by Louise and Dennis' standards, each stood too close to the other. The lawns were covered with neatly manicured grass, arrays of colored flowers, and fruit bearing trees. There were picket fences around the yards giving the atmosphere a cozy effect.

"Doesn't this remind you of the houses in town back at home, Dennis?" Louise asked. Her comment was more of an appraisal rather than a question.

"Kind of," he responded taking in more of the street. "What I like is the fact that we won't have to go too far to the store, and the bus line is only a few blocks away."

The middle-aged woman returned and instructed them to follow her around the house to the back. She had a garden with neatly planted rows of green beans, tomatoes, and lettuce.

Louise commented, "What a lovely vegetable garden," while stopping to admire it.

"Thanks honey, you said your name is Louise?"

"Yes ma'am."

"Louise, I grew up on a farm outside of Pine Bluff, Arkansas. I enjoy growing my own vegetables."

"You've done a good job ma'am," complimented Louise again. The flavoring of her southern brogue came through in her speech.

Taking an immediate predilection to the couple, Mrs. Caldwell assessed that their "freshness off the farm" ambiance and innocence reminded her much of herself years ago. She observed how well they complemented and depended on each other.

Feeling comfortable in their presence, she confided, "I've lived on this property only five years. My husband was killed in a car accident, involving a freight truck. I received a settlement and was able to buy this place. It had been vacant for a few years, apparently the former owners died or moved or deserted it. The city took it over for back taxes and put it on the market for sale. I've turned it into two apartments and use the attic on the third floor for storage," explained Mrs. Caldwell.

At the end of the yard stood an old gray one-story framed house with a peaked roof with three windows facing the yard, badly in need of a paint job. It was tucked away behind a thick overgrowth of bushes and weeds. The young couple followed Mrs. Caldwell to the side entrance where she produced a key from her smock pocket and opened the double doors. The rooms were filled with old equipment, garden tools, long forgotten furniture, and pictures entwined with cobwebs and layers upon layers of dust. Streaks of daylight filtered through the windows revealing dust particles, which danced across its light.

Observing the couple's reaction, Mrs. Caldwell said, "Now I warned you about this place, and my feelings won't be hurt if you don't want to take it."

"No, no, we want it!" Louise quickly responded with foresight, planning how she would clean and arrange the house. "We aren't afraid of a little dust."

"Little, *ain't* the word for this place, child," Mrs. Caldwell declared in a robust laugh.

Dennis' scrutiny of the structure caused him to say fastidiously, "This building seems to be solidly built. It's a shame that it has been neglected."

"I agree with you. I didn't know what I was going to do with it," replied Mrs. Caldwell.

"Ma'am how many rooms are in here?"

"Four rooms with running water, but the pipes have not been used in years. When the city installed electricity on this block, they brought the electricity to the house and the circuit box is outside behind it. I never had the electricity installed, so you will have to use candles until we can have someone install it."

Louise made an odd gesture by crinkling up her nose at Dennis.

Grasping her hand and smiling, he reassured her, "I can install electricity in no time Lou, I promise."

"I'll gladly pay for the material you will need," said Mrs. Caldwell.

Dennis asked, "What do you want us to do with this stuff?" motioning with his hand while he looked around.

"Except for my gardening tools you can discard all of it. It belonged to the people that lived here years before I moved in."

"Where can I put the things we don't want?"

"In the alley behind the house, garbage pickup day is on Wednesdays. Come on, let me show you the back."

The back of the coach house also had three windows which faced the alley. The center of the yard was clear but there were more discarded things in the yard along the wooden picket fence. The yard extended about fifty feet back to the alley and there was an apple tree off to one side. Louise's curiosity concerning the building made her attention linger upon it.

As if Mrs. Caldwell could read her thoughts, she said, "This was probably a coach house at one time because I think my house was one of the first on this block."

"What's a coach house?" Louise innocently asked.

Dennis explained, "Lou, a coach house is a separate place where servants lived, and it could've housed carriages and horses."

"Oh, that's interesting, it's something like a citified barn," she chuckled, and the air was coupled with their laughter.

"May I plant my own garden back here and eat the apples from the tree?" Louise asked.

"You can do whatever you like, just save me some of the apples."

"It's a deal then," remarked Dennis.

"Is that your pickup truck in the front of the house?" Mrs. Caldwell asked.

"Yes ma'am," replied Dennis.

"You can drive it around here, unload, and park it next to the fence. Nobody will bother it."

"Thanks."

As his eyes wandered over to a stack of wood he asked, "Can I build you a new shed for your garden tools with that wood over there?"

"Do you think you'll have time?

"Sure I'll make time ma'am, I'll have it up in a few days, if that's alright with you? How about if I pay you for the month? That'll be one less thing I'll have to be concerned about."

Overjoyed with his statement she concurred, "That's fine with me. I'd like to advise you, if you need the services of a banking facility, there's a bank a few blocks over. It isn't wise for you to be carrying large amounts of money around in your pockets."

"Thanks for the advice, but we don't have much money ma'am," Dennis replied.

"Just remember what I said," she advised, giving them the key to the building before returning to her house.

5

Louise rushed into Dennis' open arms to receive a warm embrace.

Gazing into her eyes, he said, "Lou, this is *gonna* take a lot of work. With me starting on a new job tomorrow morning, it's *gonna* be left up to you during the day, but I will help when I get home. Do you think you can handle this?"

Rolling her eyes at him with her hands on her hips and patting her foot, she scolded, "Now Dennis, since when have I been afraid of work? Have you forgotten that I grew up on a working farm, and I also lived with your family and the women took care of the house and farm work, while you guys were off somewhere? God only knows what you were doing when you were supposed to be on a construction job."

Loving the sassy manner in which she moved her head when making a point, he wrapped her in his arms and kissed her lips. "That's why I love you, we're good for one another," he expressed.

It was early in the afternoon. They unloaded some of the contents of their truck in the backyard before heading to the grocery and hardware stores. In the supermarket, they purchased cleaning items and food to last for a few days. At the hardware store, they purchased gallons of white paint, paint supplies, buckets, candles, and had another key made. Dennis inquired about the electrical wiring requirements and perused the items he needed for installing electricity. Louise insisted on buying some lye to make a strong soap and a couple of mousetraps.

Dennis argued, "Why do you need to get mousetraps? I didn't see any mice."

"That doesn't mean they aren't there. Besides, I saw their droppings. I am not going to live in a place with mice if I can help it,"
she responded, refusing to relinquish her mission.

Their last stop was the gas station to pick up more ice.

Within an hour and a half, they were back at their new place,
unloading the truck and conducting a massive clean up campaign.
Among the things in the house were tables, chairs, and pictures they
decided to keep. The oil and oil burning lamps they found would be
useful since they did not have electricity. They also found cooking
utensils and tools that they felt would be of some value to them. In
the kitchen was a working gas stove, which Louise scrubbed until it
was clean and in no time, she was able to make a batch of soap on it.
After several hours of rigorous work they cleared out the place,
cleaned the walls and ceilings.

"A fresh coat of paint will make these rooms look nice don't you
think?" asked Dennis.

"Yes, it would indeed. We can do that later. I'm hungry, how
about you?"

"The word food sounds good. Why don't I bring in our things,
while you start dinner?"

)0(

Sitting in the kitchen at an old wooden table that they found in
the house, they ate their first meal of catfish, potatoes, and sweet
corn.

"Lou, dinner is delicious. You amaze me at how quickly you
adapt to new situations. You didn't hesitate for a moment about
digging in and helping when you joined me and my family and now
taking charge of what needs to be done around here," complimented Dennis."

"Thanks Dennis."

They spent the evening discussing their plans for the house and the yard.

"I need to call Henry and let him know that we are here. I saw a pay phone a couple of blocks away."

"It's so late, maybe you should wait until tomorrow."

"No, I don't want him to worry about us."

)0(

"Hello, Henry. Is that you?" asked Dennis in an amiable tone.

"Yeah it's me. Dennis Clark! Man, I'd know your voice anywhere. Where are you?" he asked, in an undeniable southern drawl.

"Lou and I arrived this morning. I lucked out, found a job, and a place to stay."

"Oh yeah, where?"

"On Iroquois and Stewart Streets."

After giving Henry the address, Henry said he and his wife would be over the following evening. Dennis rushed home to share the news with his wife.

Together the couple put up their bed. Dennis ran himself a well-deserved bath in their porcelain tub, while Louise put away their clothes in a chest of drawers they brought with them.

She shouted to him, "You'd better appreciate the scrubbing I did to get that tub clean!"

"Believe me, I do!" he shouted back.

Once he finished his bath, he ran water for Louise, and by the time, she reached the bedroom, he was sound asleep. Taking a few moments to reflect by looking around, Louise admired their promising new home. Before blowing out the lanterns and candles, she leaned over to kiss her husband goodnight.

In the darkness, she heard some scampering on the floor. "Oh no you don't," she whispered. Rising to relight the lantern, she went in search of her new mousetraps. She set them with bread, one in the kitchen and the other in the bedroom before going back to bed.

6

Dennis woke up first. Heading for the bathroom on his bare feet, he noticed a dead mouse in a trap. Chuckling to himself, he deliberated, *the woman was right.* He went to the kitchen to find something to chuck it out in, where he discovered the second trap filled with another stiff creature. Disposing of both of them and resetting the traps, he washed up and dressed for work. His movements made Louise stir. He went over to kiss her.

"Good morning Lou, how did you sleep?"

"Great, but do you have to get up so early?" she said drowsily, stretching her arms and legs.

"I've got to go to work, have you forgotten?"

"No, what time is it?"

"Five thirty. Can you rustle me up some breakfast and something for lunch? I have to be there at seven."

"Sure Dennis," she said, as she rose focusing her eyes immediately on her trap. "Hum," she replied, "no mouse? I thought I'd catch one for sure."

"Catch what?" replied Dennis mocking her.

"A mouse silly, can't you see I set a trap?"

"I told you there weren't any mice."

She got up and examined her trap, then went into the kitchen and scrutinized the second trap. There were tell tale marks left on her traps, plus they were moved from their original spots. Louise turned to shout for Dennis, but he stood behind her laughing.

"Okay, you caught two," he admitted. "I got rid of them before you woke up."

"See, I told you!" she said laughing hardily, while shaking her finger at him.

She prepared breakfast for the both of them and packed a nice lunch of homemade bread, ham, and fresh apples for Dennis.

"I put some ice and fresh water in the jug for you to drink," she informed him as she kissed him goodbye. "Good luck on your first day. Please be careful going up in that elevator."

Walking to his truck, he shouted over his shoulder to her, "Love you gal!"

)0(

Since their friends were coming over at six thirty, Louise started her day out by painting the kitchen, living room, and bathroom so the house would look a little more presentable. Opening all the windows and leaving the doors open allowed the house to air out. By mid-afternoon, she hung and adjusted curtains that her mother-in-law had given her.

)0(

As Dennis neared the entrance to the house, he smelled paint. "Hi hon," he said as he curiously ventured through the house, taking in Louise's paint job while she followed him around to see what his reaction was going to be. He smiled before saying, "You've been busy, I see."

"Do you like what I've done?" she asked with enthusiasm.

"Well, yes, you've done a good job."

Scrutinizing the living room, he could see that the paint was not applied evenly on the walls and there were splatters of it all over the floor.

"Where *is* the paint and the paint thinner?" he asked.

"They're in the backroom, why?"

I just need to touch up the paint a little."

"So, you don't like my paint job!" she said sarcastically.

With no aspiration to hurt his wife's feelings, diplomatically he said, "its okay Lou, but it's not even. Sometimes that's the hardest thing to do when you paint. Let me just paint over this quickly before Henry and Tammy come over."

Louise rolled her eyes and complained, "You're not the only one who can paint."

"Of course not. Please don't get mad, sweetheart."

"Don't you dare try to sweet talk your way out of this mister!"

Dennis laughed and teased her by kissing her neck before he started repainting the rooms. While Dennis painted and cleaned up the floors, she ran him a tub of hot water to bathe in and continued preparing their supper.

)0(

Henry and his wife, Tammy, lived approximately twenty minutes away and arrived by six o'clock.

"My, it's so good to see you after all this time. Let me look at you," said Tammy with her contagious jovial personality, turning Louise completely around. She stood about four feet ten inches tall and wore her hair in a layered curled fashion with a tapered back.

"There's something different about you though," she continued.

"Just give me a hug," said Louise, "it's good to see you."

While the women embraced each other, the men exchanged big bear hugs. "Man, oh man, I finally got my best buddy to come and join me," said Henry in a boisterous tone. He and Dennis stood equal in height, but Henry's muscles were more developed.

Pointing to the couple with a tilt of her head, Tammy said, "Henry, look at them. I know what's different. They both have put on some weight."

Yep, I recognize the look of 'love,'" said Henry over emphasizing his pronunciation of the word love.

"You know when you're content and in 'love' you pick up extra pounds," teased Tammy with hardy laughter.

"Look at yourselves, you've done the same," rebutted Louise.

"Well, I have more of an excuse," defended Tammy.

"Where are your twins? asked Louise.

"We left them with our next door neighbor. She's a wonderful lady who's crazy about them," remarked Tammy.

Louise set the table, while Dennis showed the couple their new home. She prepared red beans, rice, and fried chicken, adding homemade bread and relish she brought from home. They served their first dinner with their guests in the kitchen on the aged wooden table and chairs that came with the house. Louise decorated the table with a pale green tablecloth, which added a sense of homeliness to the room.

Henry stood as he toasted the new couple, "Welcome!" he said, turning to each of them, "to Los Angeles, the city for new adventures. I can guarantee you're *gonna* love it here."

"Here, here!" Tammy added, as they all clicked their bottles of beer together.

Tammy commented, "Guys, you worked fast, the paint makes this place look new. I bet your landlord will be surprised."

"I plan on inviting her over tomorrow for some apple fritters," said Louise.

"She'll be impressed with your cooking too. Dinner is good, Lou," complimented Dennis.

"Thanks Dennis."

Louise and Dennis became absorbed in the stories Henry and Tammy shared with them regarding Los Angeles. They were genuinely pleased that their friends had done so well. Henry worked for the city and Tammy worked in a metal fabrication factory. Both couples went to school together in Avinger. They rekindled their friendship by trading childhood stories over bottles of beer that Tammy and Henry brought with them.

Tammy helped Louise clean the kitchen, while the guys went outside to smoke aromatic cigars. Shortly afterward, the couple departed and Henry promised to return on Saturday to help paint the building's exterior.

After their friends left, Dennis quickly changed into some old clothes and started painting the backroom.

"Oh Dennis, that's enough work for one day," announced Louise at ten thirty.

"No it's not. If I don't do it, you'll attempt to do it. I know you won't wait until I get home."

"Are you saying I can't paint and would do a messy job?" she ridiculed.

"Yep, that's exactly what I'm saying," he sniggered.

Louise joined him, he showed her how to use the paintbrushes, and together they finished painting the inside of the house.

)0(

The next morning after Dennis left for work, Louise made a mental list of the work she needed to perform. After cleaning the kitchen, she felt fatigued and decided to take a little nap before tackling anything else. Dozing off to sleep, she acknowledged to herself that leaving Avinger was an adventure she initially rejected, but thus far, things were working out.

Awakening refreshed she went in the backyard to see what was salvageable. There was a worn couch with two matching chairs. The stuffing in them was intact but they were extremely filthy. Pouring some hot water into a bucket, she added a batch of soap made from the lye. After scrubbing and soaking the furniture from top to bottom, Louise stepped back and marveled at the revitalized furniture.

Positioning them so they would receive the full benefit of the warm sun to help them dry, she dabbed them with some of her scented rose water cologne to make them smell nice and fresh.

She found several empty wooden crates and gave them a good cleansing. *These will be useful for storing things and maybe if Dennis has time he can make drawers to fit into them,* she contemplated. Assiduously finding things to use, she ran across a worn carpet, cut and salvaged two pieces from it, cleaned them, and hung them over the fence to dry. Later she planned on putting them on the floor on each side of the bed.

In one of the crates were rolls of old wallpaper and paste. Forcefully opening the jar of paste, she sniffed at it and tested it by dipping her finger in it to determine whether it was still good. Nodding her head with satisfaction, she cleaned the wallpaper then pasted it on the walls of the pantry and the bedroom closets. With the extra wallpaper, she lined the wooden crates, carried six of them into the second bedroom, and stacked them on their sides in two columns, resolving that Dennis could use them to store his tools. Her inquisitiveness made her wonder what the crates had housed.

)0(

By mid-afternoon, she found tools and miscellaneous items that they could use. In each room, with nails, wire, and hammer in hand, she hung and adjusted curtains that her mother-in-law had given her. Subsequently, she hung some of the family pictures they brought with them as well as some of the framed scenic pictures that came with the house. Not wanting to discard anything without Dennis seeing it first, she left the rest of the loot in the yard. The couch and chairs were nearly dry so she got two boys that were passing by in the alley to help her carry them into the house. Louise rewarded them with candy, and they left happily. The couch was situated so it faced the back windows with the view of the yard facing the alley. Placing two crates upside down in front of the couch and covering them with a tablecloth added a nice touch of permanence. She arranged the two remaining crates by the matching chairs so that they would serve as occasional tables. *I'll be glad when Dennis installs electricity so we won't have to use these oil lamps,* she thought, placing one each on her makeshift end tables. She took a rug her mother had given her and placed it on the wooden floor in front of the couch, but soon discovered she liked it better underneath her newly made cocktail table.

Tirelessly, Louise picked apples for her fritters, washed them, and started to make her dough. "Darn, I don't have enough butter," she said out loud. Checking her purse for money, she walked out the front to go to the store.

Mrs. Caldwell poked her head out of her door. "Hi Louise, how is everything going?"

"Good afternoon Mrs. Caldwell, everything is just fine. I'd like for you to stop by later to see what I've been doing, if you have time."

"Sure thing, where are you headed?"

"I'm going to the store, do you need anything?"

"I could use some bread and a dozen eggs. Do you mind getting them for me?"

"Of course not."

"Please wait here while I go get some money," responded Mrs. Caldwell.

7

It was springtime. Although in southern California it was always hot, a light breeze kicked up, making the long stem branches of a weeping willow tree dance slowly in the wind. Louise watched as an occasional leaf trickled to the ground. A neighbor working in her yard greeted her as she passed and they exchanged pleasantries. Two small children were playing in their yard as their mother stood watching them. Louise waved at the mother and received a friendly wave in return. Her experiences were no different from being at home in the country, *Home is where your heart is,* she decided. Her new haven felt safe and secure.

The shopping area was a few blocks away and the street was filled with stores of all sorts. To save time, Louise cut through the parking lot of the A & P grocery store on the corner. Across the street was the hardware store she and Dennis visited the day before. Next to it, was a drugstore, cleaners, and fabric shop. On the next block, there were doctor and dentist offices, clothing stores, a bank, and a restaurant. Further down the street were more restaurants, a cinema, bowling alley, and other businesses essential to the neighborhood. Within a three-block radius, there were enough shops to sustain customers without them having to leave the community.

If they would ever get the opportunity to buy a house, she wanted one in this same neighborhood. Finding amusement in her thoughts, knowing Dennis, he would not want to buy a house. With his grandiose ideas, he would probably want to build one. Chortling to herself, *Maybe one day he will.*

Subsequent to choosing the items she needed in the grocery store, Louise walked across the street to look in the fabric shop. The shop was filled with customers and the proprietor could not keep up with them. She waited patiently until he was able to direct his attention to her.

"May I help you miss?" he asked.

"How much is a yard of this cloth?" she asked holding a bolt of material in her arms.

Examining it, he told her the price and she purchased two yards.

"From the looks of things sir, you need someone to help you here. Would you consider hiring me?"

"Hum, let me give it some thought. Do you have a phone number where I can reach you?"

"No, I just moved here from Texas, and I haven't had a chance to have a phone installed. How about me checking back with you in a day or so?"

"Sounds good, what is your name?"

"Louise, sir."

"I thought I recognized a Texan accent. My wife's family lives in San Antonio. Do you have any experience working in a store?"

"Sure do," she fibbed. "I worked in my mother-in-law's bakery. Although food and cloth isn't the same, you're still selling a product to a customer. The way you treat the customers is what matters," she added.

The storeowner smiled.

"I can't pay much, but how does $15.00 a week sound?"

"That's fine," Louise replied, trying not to sound too elated.

"When can you start?"

"I can start on Monday."

"It's a deal, be here by nine thirty. I'm Mr. Hirsch, glad to meet you," extending his hand in a firm handshake to seal their deal.

Filled with excitement and broadly grinning Louise replied, "The pleasure is all mine sir. See you on Monday."

)0(

Euphoric, because of her good fortune, this was her first real job that did not pertain to farming, cooking, or cleaning. Until she got married and moved in with Dennis' family, she did not do anything that she considered mind stimulating. Her mother-in-law, Mary, encouraged independent thinking and demonstrated to her how to develop her ideas. Once Mary realized she was a proficient seamstress, she commissioned her to a make a fancy dress for her to wear at a church social. Mary received so many compliments on the dress that Louise received orders from some of the other ladies to make dresses for them.

Kristin, one of Dennis' younger sisters, needed a new dress for her music recital. She was playing a piece on the piano by Chopin, and she wanted a replica of a costume that the ladies wore in the early 1800's. Mary thought it was ridiculous to make something that elaborate, only to be worn once, but Kristin insisted. She and Louise worked hard selling pastries, fruit, and vegetables to make the money to purchase the fabric needed for the costume. Kristin had a picture from a book of the dress she wanted. Louise made it for her on Mary's sewing machine. On the morning of the recital, Louise and Kristin locked themselves up in Kristin's room and did not reappear until it was time to leave. Exiting the room, Kristin looked superb in her costume, with her hair pinned up with curls dangling on the sides. Carrying a fan she made, Kristin pretended as if she was one of the elegant ladies of that era. At the recital, she received a standing ovation for playing the piano in her fancy costume.

Mary Clark taught Louise to monopolize and improve upon the things she did. "Strive to do your best at whatever you do," she told

Louise. Louise had never met a woman like Mary, and she idolized her. Her own parents taught her good morals and about farming, with her mother placing emphasis on feminine things. Mary focused on survival in a broader sense, stimulation of the mind, digging within the depths of her soul and bringing out her potential. She watched how Mary and John Clark related to their children. They expected superlative performance from all of them and received it in return. She admired that same drive in Dennis and felt they were perfectly matched.

)0(

In exhilaration, Louise practically skipped back to her house from the fabric store.

Running up the stairs to give Mrs. Caldwell her goods and change she blurted out, "Guess what?"

With a look of concern on her face Mrs. Caldwell inquired, "What child, is something wrong?"

"Oh no ma'am, I just got a job."

"*Landsake*, where?"

"*Ohhh*, at Mr. Hirsch's fabric store," she replied. She could not stand still long enough as she jumped joyously up and down.

"That's right, his wife just recently suffered a heart attack. I'm sure he can use the help. I'm happy for you."

"Thank you Mrs. Caldwell. I need to start my dinner, can you come back to see what we've done in about an hour?"

"Sure can, I'll see you later," she said cheerfully.

Rushing to open the door, she was not aware of the two strangers who were lurking in the alley observing her entrance into her house. She put her things down, washed her hands, and made her dough for her apple fritters. After finishing, she started dinner, quickly putting away some of the remaining things they had brought from home. By the time Mrs. Caldwell knocked on the door her dinner was done. Welcoming her into her new home, she stood in the background proudly watching Mrs. Caldwell's reaction to the revitalized coach house.

"My goodness child, this doesn't even have the slightest resemblance of the way it looked before. You and that good-looking husband of yours have done a miraculous job in changing this place almost overnight! I think I am going to have to charge you more rent," she teased good-naturedly. Taking her seriously, wrinkled lines of worry formed across Louise's brow. Immediately, Mrs. Caldwell replied, "I was just kidding, child, I didn't mean to upset you," giving her a reassuring hug. "Show me the rest of your place." In awe, the older woman visited each room. "Where did you get all this stuff?"

"Believe it or not, most of it was already here. Dennis hasn't seen all the work I have done," Louise added with enthusiasm.

As they returned to the kitchen, Mrs. Caldwell said, "I have a refrigerator in the attic that you can have, after your husband hooks up the electricity."

"Oh thank you, we'd be so grateful," Louise responded. "Now, I have something for you." Opening the oven, she produced a plate with several apple fritters. "I made these just for you. Try one."

Biting into the mouth-watering pastry, Mrs. Caldwell smiled as she ate. "This is wonderful! Did you use the apples from the tree in the back?"

"Sure did, and I have a sack of them for you."

"Those apples never tasted this good for me. Thank you Louise. Let me get out of here before your husband comes home. Your surprises for him should be special, just between you and him."

)0(

Periodically, Louise watched out the living room window around the time she expected Dennis home. Upon his arrival, she greeted him at the door. Eagerly covering his eyes with her hands, she insisted that he keep his eyes closed.

"I have a surprise for you. Promise you won't try to look."

"Okay, what do you want me to do?"

Her jovial disposition overflowed onto him.

"Let me guide you to the bathroom and promise not to look."

"I promise."

Allowing her to lead him to the bathroom, he found a hot bath and fresh clothes waiting for him.

"What have you been up to?" he asked with curiosity.

"You'll see, just take your bath," she replied with an intriguing air. "Put your dirty clothes in this basket," Louise said as she pointed to it. His cheerful grins demonstrated his happiness with her ingenuity. "And use some of this rose water cologne," she ordered.

"I don't want to use that girly smelly stuff!" he retorted.

"Didn't you buy it for me because you liked the way it smelled?"

"Yeah, but on you."

"I like the way it smells on us, now use it, please."

"Only for you in the privacy of our home will I ever use it, do you understand?" he said, conceding because he did not want to spoil her surprise.

"After you finish, call me so I can come and get you."

)0(

"Are you ready?" shouted Louise from the front of the house, after quickly placing the food on the table and lighting the candles. Meeting Dennis at the bathroom door and sniffing at him, she commented, "Boy do you smell good." Slapping her bottom, he followed her.

Opening the door to the first room, she announced, "We can store tools and miscellaneous items in here until you build a shed for them. Later we can change it into an extra bedroom."

"Lou, you've done a great job organizing my tools," he said impressed with her utilization of the crates.

Following her into their bedroom and inspecting the room, he again complimented her handiwork. In the living room, he stood and looked inquisitively around the room before he said, "This isn't the same furniture we hauled out of here yesterday, is it? I don't recall it looking this good, or did you get it from Mrs. Caldwell?"

"No, it's the very same furniture. I cleaned it and aired it out. It's still damp but should be dry by tomorrow."

"It looks good Lou. How did you get it back in here?"

"I paid two boys to help me bring it in, and they accepted candy for their services."

"Crates for tables? Who would have ever thought about using them this way?"

"Dennis, what do you think they were used for?"

Scratching the back of his head, he replied, "Hon, they're the kind of crates you'd use for shipping goods on a ship. They are heavily constructed because they need to be able to endure rough treatment and water. They could have been used for shipping bottles of wines, cloth, or guns, or just about anything."

"I'm proud with what you have done here, you ought to be tired," he said, pulling her close to him and kissing her before asking, "What's for dinner?"

"Typical man, always wanting something to eat," she teased.

During their meal, Dennis filled Louise in on what he had been doing all day.

"The work isn't hard, you just have to be strong. I like what I'm doing, and I'll be learning different aspects of construction."

"Did you inform your boss that you are a professional carpenter?"

"Yes, I told him yesterday and mentioned it again today. His name is Warren Stern, and he told me I will be given a chance to prove it when the time comes."

"Good, don't forget to mention it then."

"Don't worry Lou, I know what to do," he persisted, as if she were indulgencing him as a child.

"Guess what else I did today?" said Louise, bursting to share her news.

"I have no idea. What did you do?"

"I went to the material store and bought some fabric for a new tablecloth and the shop owner hired me. I'll start work on Monday."

Privately, Dennis was delighted that Louise was making a quick transition to a different way of life, because he feared she would want to return home to their family. Openly he expressed, "That's wonderful! Things are happening fast for us, I think we'll do just fine."

After they finished eating, Louise put on a short pot of coffee to serve with dessert. She urged him up and suggested they go out in the backyard for some fresh air while the coffee brewed. He followed his lovely young wife to the pile of remaining things they had removed from the house.

"Dennis, I didn't want to discard any of this stuff until you got a chance to go through it, because there may be something here you can use."

Picking up a couple pieces of pipe and a crowbar he said, "I can use most of this stuff and that's probably the reason for it being stored in the house. I need to protect it though if it rains. Where did we put that tarpaulin?"

Louise shrugged her shoulders and pointed to the pile.

"I'll dig it out and use it to cover up this stuff until I have time to thoroughly go through it and sort it out. Tomorrow evening after work, I'll build the shed for Mrs. Caldwell's garden tools."

"You also promised me electricity."

"I know Lou, give me some time," he pleaded.

"Come on, the coffee is ready by now."

After eating their dessert of apple fritters, Louise helped Dennis find the tarpaulin and they secured it over the pile. "Let's go to bed," Lou urged, "I've got an itch for you to scratch."

)0(

Louise listened to Dennis snore, while he slept. Unwavering in his plan to leave Texas and make a new life for them, she could not imagine why he wanted to leave their families and work in a foreign place doing the same kind of work that he could do at home. Acquiescing as his wife, she vowed to share his dreams and in her desire to please him, she decided that she would help him in whatever way she could.

8

Their morning routine was established, whereas Dennis got up for work first, and Louise made breakfast and lunch for him. After he went to work, she would go back to bed for an additional hour or two. This particular morning, she deliberated, *Since I'll be starting work on Monday, I'd better enjoy this luxury while I can.* She remained in bed for a while longer.

)0(

Dressed in green baggy pants, a floral smock, and a straw hat that had seen better days, Mrs. Caldwell was on her knees working in her garden when Louise exited the house. *It looks fitting for her to be here, just like my ma at home,* Louise decided.

"Good morning Louise. How are things going?" Mrs. Caldwell asked.

"Very well Mrs. Caldwell. How are you today?"

"Just fine my dear. I'm weeding out my garden. I work out here almost every other day."

Redirecting her attention to the coach house Louise said, "Well, I'm going to remove some of the vegetation that has grown around the house so that we can paint on Saturday."

"I used to be like you when I was fresh off the farm, hard work meant nothing," remarked Mrs. Caldwell.

)0(

Concentrating on the job at hand, Louise dug out overgrown bushes with tools from her house, trimmed branches, and raked leaves before washing the sides of the house with her special soap. Thoughtfully, Mrs. Caldwell observed her, and when Louise took a break, she approached her.

"Here are two cans of yellow paint that was left over from when the house was painted last year. The cans have been opened and resealed, but the paint should still be good," she said.

"Thank you, now the coach house will match yours," said Louise.

When Louise finished, she bathed and took a leisurely walk around the neighborhood, opposite the direction of the stores. She wandered across an elementary school, and a grassy park with a playground, a sand box, and a baseball field. On her way back home, Louise took a different route. Discovering a library, she ventured inside. *This building is two stories tall, much larger than the library at home.* The second floor housed books for adults. When Louise reached the top of the stairs, she was amazed by the huge selection. There were rows of books, the likes of nothing she had seen before. Incredulously, she walked down the aisles, discovering the various sections and memorizing their locations. *This is going to be my favorite place.* Taking her time, she perused each aisle before deciding on a few books. With the assistance of a friendly librarian, she obtained a library card, a list of the events for the month, and borrowed several books. Upon her return home, she made herself comfortable on the bed and started reading one of her books.

)0(

"My, my, haven't *we* been busy today," said Dennis standing over Louise with a big grin on his face.

"Gosh Dennis, I haven't even started dinner." Louise stretched as she yarned. "I was reading and must have fallen asleep."

"That's okay Lou. I promised Mrs. Caldwell that I would build the shed for her garden tools. I can work on that while you prepare dinner."

"Dennis, aren't you tired from working all day?"

"No Lou, the work I did today was easy."

While Dennis worked on his construction project, Louise fried catfish, made spaghetti, Johnnycakes, and prepared a relish plate. The mouth-watering aroma of the food cooking permeated the outdoors, stirring under Dennis nostrils, causing him to poke his head in the door.

"It sure smells good in here, how much longer will it be before dinner is ready?"

"Come on in now and wash up, dinner will be ready in about ten minutes."

During their meal, they shared the events of the day. Louise listened intently to Dennis' enthusiastic explanation of his new duties. "There will be thirty floors, and I'm working on the fifth floor," he said proudly, making gestures with his hands. Comfortable with his new job, he was not overtaxed and enjoyed being around the people he worked with. It was spellbinding for him working on a new building that would eventually be used for office space. As he spoke, Louise's mind wandered, thinking he would be happy no matter where he went, especially with his easygoing demeanor. While he cherished adventure and meeting new people, she was just the opposite and found contentment in things that were familiar. For the time being, she found solace in their new home, in the relationship she was forming with Mrs. Caldwell, and now the library.

Returning outside after their meal, Louise watched Dennis continue his work on the shed. Upon its completion, Mrs. Caldwell appeared in the yard singing his praises for the miraculous job he had done in such a short time.

As they stood looking at it, Dennis said, "When I go to the hardware store, I'll buy a padlock for the door. I'll paint it and the coach house tomorrow."

"You just earned yourself a month's free rent, besides I want you two to stick around, you're enriching my life," said Mrs. Caldwell.

Dennis winked at Louise, as they exchanged smiles of satisfaction.

Two men exited from the back of Mrs. Caldwell's house.

"Hello," they greeted in unison. "What's all the commotion about?" asked the oldest man in his early fifties.

"We're admiring the new shed Dennis just finished building. I'm overjoyed with his work," said Mrs. Caldwell.

"Paul and Mark Nielsen, I would like for you to meet my other new tenants, Dennis and Louise Clark."

The men shook hands with Dennis, but Louise backed off only nodding her head at them. Mrs. Caldwell added, "Mark is Paul's son, and they're moving in now." The men were white, which surprised Dennis because he was not expecting whites to rent from a black lady. Dennis rationalized that they were in California, therefore, things were done in a different manner. Louise, on the other hand felt ill at ease, she did not like the up and down scrutiny, she received from both men. Finding them objectionable, she refused to shake their hands.

Paul, the older man with a discernible appearance was blonde and rather handsome, even though his face was unshaven. He possessed the bluest eyes that Louise had ever seen. His stance was so upright that she imagined him with a board in the back of his clothes. He had a medium physique with the faintest hint of a protruding belly. His son, Mark was slim with dark hair and keen features and he did not have the slightness resemblance to his father. There was something odd about him. Perhaps it was the ruthless way he stared or his creepy unkempt appearance, infrequently scratching at his crotch.

Accepting them without any qualms Dennis asked, "What kind of work do you *fellas* do?"

Paul answered, "We travel a lot for the Pacific-Atlantic Railroad."

"Mrs. Caldwell," said Paul, "we just finished bringing in the last of our things. I didn't know you had two places for rent."

"I didn't actually, but when Dennis told me he was a carpenter and that he and Louise didn't mind cleaning up the coach house, I decided to rent it out to them."

Taken aback by her statement, the men glanced quickly at each other.

Paul said, "I wish you had told us about the place, *cause* we would have been interested in taking it…uh, so we wouldn't have to disturb you when we come and go. Which may be at odd times of the night," he quickly added.

"Yeah, we are handymen too," said Mark. "Sure wish you had told us about the coach house first."

Paul nudged Mark to shut up. No one noticed this exchange but Louise.

"If you need any help cleaning up your place we sure would like to help *ya*," commented Paul.

"No thanks! We don't need your help!" interjected Louise in a brusque tone that caused Dennis to gawk at her strangely.

"I'd love to see your place if you don't mind," said Paul.

His speech was coupled with charisma and wit as he directed his attention to Dennis, consciously aware that Louise did not care for him. "Me too. *Haennnnn!*" said his son. Mark had an irritating form of laughter. It was a nervous laugh used to fill in an awkward silence. The sound reminded you of the cartoon character, Porky Pig. He would make a smart remark and end or begin it with, "*Haennnnn!*"

Sensing that Louise was about to reply in an obnoxious manner, Dennis stepped forward, saying, "Perhaps another time, I've got to go and clean up." Snatching and practically dragging Louise behind him, they bid their farewells, rushing toward their house.

"Nice looking woman. *Haennnnn!*" commented Mark taking in Louise's backside as they hurried away.

"Behave yourself! We must respect the ladies," warned Paul with a menacing gaze.

Mrs. Caldwell chuckled, "He's just kidding around like any young man."

Mark snuggled next to Mrs. Caldwell holding his head down, looking out from under his eyes, and blinking his eyelashes with the innocence of a child. The effect turned her to mush. "You are such a dear young man," she commented.

Upon entering the house, Dennis howled, "I didn't like your attitude. Your behavior was atrocious, and it was certainly uncalled for!"

"I don't like those men. They were both looking at me as if they were undressing me on the spot. Their breath reeked of alcohol and I feel there is some underlying reason for them moving in this neighborhood. The only whites I have seen are the storeowners. Why are they so interested in moving in here, specifically here?" she spoke rapidly. "They're up to no good. I don't want them sniffing around here, do you understand?" she shouted, her chest heaving from anger.

"I am sure they are okay."

"No, they aren't! Don't you dare invite them into my house!"

"Your house! This is our house! Don't worry! I won't invite them in here because I can't trust you to treat them cordially! And stop raising your voice at me! I have never seen you act like this before!"

Other than the few arguments they had in high school, there was never a major disagreement between them. This was the first time

Louise dared to exhibit an ill-tempered disposition, which was so foreign to her usual mild manner that Dennis was truly perplexed by it. Later that evening in their bed, he attempted to calm Louise's salty temperament, but she was in no mood to be bothered.

9

Saturday morning Louise woke up in a better frame of mind. With a great deal of circumspect, Dennis avoided mentioning the other tenants. "We need to call home and let everyone know we made it safely," he mentioned to her. Driving to a pay phone a couple of blocks away, they called Louise's parents to report their arrival. "We both have jobs Mama," Louise said, her happiness projected through the phone. She spent several minutes reporting to her parents about their good fortune. Her mother, Anna Mae, was inwardly content as she listened to Louise's cheerful recount about their house, jobs, and the rapport Louise was establishing with her landlord. It would be Anna Mae's job to contact Dennis' family and pass along their news.

As a child, Louise could always be found timidly at her mother's skirt tails. Louise compensated her introversion by trying to appear to be outgoing, but she was more comfortable among younger children and senior citizens rather than people her own age. Spending hours in the presence of older adults, Louise would listen to their endless accounts about their lives. Their stories intrigued her. Constantly, she came home from school with tales about the children not liking her. She complained to Anna Mae that she did not seem to fit in and did not know what to talk about with her classmates. Anna Mae would comfort her by telling her to be herself. Her mother did not understand Louise's quiet nature and that she was afraid of rejection by her peers, because at home Louise did not have any trouble relating to her family and close friends.

When Anna Mae realized that Dennis was meant to be Louise's life long mate, she encouraged their relationship. Dennis was too restless and talented to mirror the efforts of just an average carpenter and farmer. He was the type of individual that took charge of things, and she would not be surprised if he would run his own company someday. A life with Dennis meant having an opportunity to do something other than being married to the soil as she was. When Louise approached her about leaving Avinger, Anna Mae wanted her to seize that opportunity because she saw how much Dennis loved her and knew he would make a great husband, father, and provider. That, she was sure of. Anna Mae also realized moving to California would be harrowing for Louise, but felt Louise needed this push to expand her personal development. She knew her daughter would be alright.

)0(

Henry arrived at Dennis and Louise's, informing them that Tammy was expecting them for dinner at their house at seven o'clock. While the men painted, Henry confided to Dennis that he worked for the Bureau of Street Services.

"Guess what division I work in?" he asked.

Dennis shrugged his shoulders.

The gesticulation made Henry reply, "The Street Tree Division."

"The What?" You mean to tell me that there is such a division. We certainly didn't call it that at home."

Bountiful laughter soared through the air. Once they stopped laughing, they looked at each other and started laughing again until tears escaped from their eyes.

"After working at the saw mill and on a farm cutting trees for lumber they figured when they hired me that I had more experience than they did. I hope to apply for a supervisory position next spring," said Henry.

"Good for you man, I'm glad you're doing well. Lou didn't want to come here. Luckily, I was able to persuade her. She is so attached to her mother, but Anna Mae surprised me and backed me up. She told her she should accompany her husband. If things work out well, maybe we can go home for Christmas. Hopefully, that will keep her pacified. I like having her here by myself, if you know what I mean?"

"Yeah man, I do. Even with our boys, Tammy and I enjoy each other's company. When I've had a hard day, she's there for me. She's understanding and knows how to soothe me," he chuckled with Dennis joining in.

Walking out of the house with two glasses of ice water in her hands, Louise asked, "And just what's so funny?" annunciating each word slowly.

"Nothing Lou, just men talk," replied Dennis, setting his jaws tight attempting to look serious. "Thanks for the water."

"I needed this, thanks Lou," replied Henry.

Suspicious of their conversation, she said, "You men gossip as much as old women."

"No we don't," replied Henry, releasing a boisterous belly chortle. Henry was solidly built with large arms and big calves, and in front of him, he carried a beer belly that shook when he laughed.

"I'll have to ask Tammy about you, mister," she replied, with her hands on her hips in an amiable fashion.

Louise decided to use some of the white paint to paint a tire and a small wooden box to use as planters for flowers. By positioning herself in their backyard, naughtily, she kept an eye on the men. Dennis and Henry's conversation conspiringly changed to baseball. By late morning, they were finished painting and Louise had lunch waiting for them.

She drove them to the hardware store for their electrical supplies after Mrs. Caldwell called the storeowner, giving her approval to have the supplies charged to her account.

Louise stated, "I need two more mousetraps, either that, or rat poison."

"For what?" asked Dennis. "You already have two traps, that's good enough."

"No it isn't," she insisted. "With two more traps, I can get rid of the mice quicker."

Dennis gave in to the traps since they were cheaper and told her to make her own poison with the lye she had. Secretly, she was going to do that anyway, but had to make it seem as if she wanted the poison in order to get him to buy her two more traps.

Henry stood shaking his head at their discussion before slyly commenting, "Dennis, you and I are going to have a lesson on the 'art of deception.' Lou has joined the ranks of the other women and has already learned about it."

"Hush!" Louise nudged him rolling her eyes.

Perfunctorily oblivious to what was going on Dennis looked from one to the other, he asked, "What?"

)0(

It took the men several hours to get the electrical wiring done. Their work involved climbing up in the crawl space in the attic, drilling holes through the ceiling, pulling wires to install outlets and fixtures in each room, and connecting the wiring to the main circuit box. The light fixtures were simple ones with bulbs and pull chains to turn them on and off. Periodically, the men tested the voltage of each line and when they finally finished, they called Louise in to test each light and outlet. Pulling each chain, she watched the rooms illuminate with light.

Giggling with joy, she praised the men, "Dennis and Henry, you've done a fine job, its wonderful having electricity! Although it was romantic using candles for a while," addressing her comment to Dennis, "there's nothing like having enough light so you don't have to strain your eyes to see! Dennis, you have one final task."

"For Pete's sake! What now Lou?"

"We need to get the refrigerator from Mrs. Caldwell's attic."

"You're a slave driver," mocked Dennis.

In no time, the refrigerator was situated in the kitchen and plugged in to see if it worked. From the reaction of Louise's face, you would have thought she was viewing one of the wonders of the world. "The humming sound of this here refrigerator is sweeter than a bird singing," she remarked. After ecstatically glazing upon it, she went and got her special soap and began cleaning it. Swollen with pride, the men stood off to the side watching her reaction. Entranced in her new mission, she forgot her manners, but quickly rectified her actions.

"Dennis and Henry, thanks again for installing the electricity and getting the refrigerator. You've worked hard today to please me. I guess now I'll allow you to rest," she ridiculed.

"Thank you, your highness," said Henry. "It was so kind of you to allow us the opportunity to serve you."

Covered with dirt, spider webs, and paint, both men playfully chased her around the kitchen table attempting to embrace her with their gratitude. Henry cleaned up a bit before Dennis walked him out to his truck. "The drinks are on me tonight. See you at seven," said Dennis.

Unbeknownst to Henry and Dennis, while they were working in the yard painting, Paul spied on them from the second floor bedroom window. To avoid suspicion he held the curtain back just enough so he could not be seen. He definitely was not going to offer his assistance because that would mean getting his hands unnecessarily dirty. Mark joined him, occasionally hoping to get a glimpse of the taboo Louise, with her shapely legs and full breasts, but she never came within his view. She was feisty and did not like him, but that did not bother him because he liked his women that way. He went out the previous night with the hope of finding some sexual relief that would put the woman temporarily out of his mind. The carousing left him with an unfulfilled desire that ended up with him beating the whore because she could not bring him to satisfaction. Surreptitiously, he vowed to get a hold of Louise and fulfill his desire for her.

10

On the way to their companions' house, Dennis and Louise stopped at the liquor store and bought soda and beer. Upon their introduction to Tammy and Henry's toddlers, the children shied away from the young couple. After an hour or so, the twins, Jacob and Jonathan adapted to Dennis and Louise by cheerfully crawling in and out of their laps. Tammy served a savory southern meal, consisting of salad, ham, greens, yams, and corn bread. Louise brought apple fritters and ice cream for dessert. As they ate, they reminisced about their hometown.

While feeding one of the twins Henry recounted, "Dennis, do you remember when we were about eight years old, my parents allowed my brother, Wally, and me to ride our bikes to your house? During the two-mile trip, we raced all the way. Wally arrived first, jumped off his bike, startling the chickens, turkeys, and geese. When he headed toward your door, that mean ole gander nibbled at his behind, grabbed his leg, and chased him around your yard! I arrived just in time to see him get bit on the butt! You were standing on your front porch laughing, and Wally was shouting for help! Your mother had to get the broom to beat the gander to make him stop pecking at him! After that, we arrived at your place in a nice quiet fashion. Your daddy thought we were so well mannered when we came to visit."

As Henry relayed the story, he sniggered and tried to keep from laughing until he finished. Dennis was egging him on because he knew the story well. Tammy and Louise had never heard it before and they laughed so hard that they both almost fell out of their chairs.

"One day my cousins, Linda, Loretta, and I were bored, so with nothing else to do we went outside and found three long sticks," started Louise. "There was a wasp hive embedded over the doorframe of the front door. Whenever you crossed the threshold, you had to dodge the wasps. Linda suggested that we should get rid of the hive once and for all. We took turns probing into it, trying to destroy it with our sticks. You should have seen those wasps stir. Since they were under attack, they did what they do best; they swarmed us! We took off in different directions and were stung three to four times each. I got stung on my nose, my scalp, and my arm, and my cousins were stung on their legs and arms. We ran across the road to our grandmother's house because my aunt was at work. Mother Sadie did not have any mercy on us. She fussed while searching for the stingers, pulling them out, and applying liniment. When I went to school everyone laughed at me because my nose was red and it swelled up twice its normal size."

"Whatever happened to the wasps?" asked Tammy.

"Our cousin, Dale smoked out the hive, getting rid of all of them. He patched up the hole with mortar so they couldn't move back in.

"I remember that," smirked Dennis, shifting in his seat and pointing his finger at her. "I called you Rudolph the red nosed reindeer."

"I know. You started everyone else calling me that too. I could have died from embarrassment. I hated you for a week after that," said Louise, as she rolled her eyes at him pouting.

"Oh baby, but you know I *loves ya*," he teased.

The evening continued with several humorous tales. This set the precedence for their biweekly gatherings.

)0(

Daylight trickled into their bedroom the next morning awakening Dennis. As his eyes adjusted to the light, he focused his attention upon Louise who was snuggled up close to him. She laid on her side with her knees slightly bent, facing him. He watched her naked bosom rise and fall as soft murmuring breaths escaped from her lips. For a brief moment, he entertained the thought of kissing and embracing her, even though he held her intimately the night before. Dennis could not get enough of her, but watching her sleep peacefully, he did not have the heart to awaken her.

He considered how fortunate he was for having such a wonderful person in his life, a wife that stood by him. He admitted to himself that he was ambitious and had several future conquests to make. Dennis asked himself, *Is it wrong for me to want more out of life?* His own mother forfeited her education to be the wife of a carpenter and farmer. He watched her juggle the duties of operating their farm, running their household, supervising the bakery, and handling the financial efforts of his father's business and their church. If his mother could find a life of contentment, then so could he.

Dennis took pride in his work and strived to build things better by going far beyond the required expectations, whenever economically possible. He was the one his father sought when it came to a new idea. Although his father used innovative techniques, Dennis' ideas were always better.

Mary Clark encouraged him to return to school and invest his time in becoming an architect, but his father was against it. John Clark felt a black man would have a hard time finding work as a degreed architect. It was difficult accepting John's way of thinking, but deep down in her soul, Mary knew he was right. That did not stop her from tackling the matter another way. She enlisted the aid of her parents and had them find a source for architectural textbooks, which they sent to Dennis. In turn, he buried himself in them, and whenever the opportunity presented itself, he applied the techniques he learned.

Rising from the bed, he carefully leaned over and lightly brushed his lips against Louise's cheek, trying not to disturb her. On his way to the bathroom, he found all four mousetraps full. *Enough is enough*, he decided, Louise had caught ten mice in the few days that they had been there. Dressing quickly, he disposed of the creatures and went on the hunt to see how they were getting into the house. *The weather is nice enough outside that they shouldn't be living in the house. Perhaps, since they are city mice they have different habits from the ones I'm used to,* he chortled and reasoned.

Checking the outside foundation, he plugged up holes with mortar and stones. He searched the floors in each room and found small crevices that the mice were using as passageways to enter the house. Remembering that there was some steel wool in one of his toolboxes, he went in search of it. Retrieving the steel wool, he plugged up the holes before plastering and painting. In the second bedroom, he found that some of the floorboards were loose. When he raised them up to see how much he needed to repair, he found a secret door that led down beneath the house. With a good deal of exertion, he pried it open. Fetching a flashlight, he descended upon the stairs and found a space the size of their living room with several shelves of gold and silver bars with Spanish lettering on them. He ran back up the stairs to gather more lanterns, returned to the secret room, and hung the lanterns on the walls so he could take in the whole room at once. The walls were made of concrete with candlestick holders mounted on them. The air was dank from water seepage on the floor. Dennis assumed the room was originally a root cellar, a storage space for vegetables like potatoes and beets. Mice scattered as the light from the lanterns acted as an illuminant against the gold and silver bars, causing the room to glow with extraordinary brilliance. He stood in the middle of the room scratching his head flabbergasted. "I'll be damned!" he said out loud.

With urgency, he rushed to Louise and found her still asleep. Rousing her he said, "Lou wake up, I found something, I want you to see!

Rising from her deep slumber, she looked curiously at him, she asked, "What time is it Dennis?"

"It's almost ten o'clock."

"It can't be! I never sleep this late."

With an uncontrollable shiver, Dennis said, "Please hurry Lou!"

11

Louise and Dennis stood astounded in the hidden cellar in the midst of the enigmatic treasure.

"Where did all of this come from? What are we going to do with it?" she asked.

"My first inclination was that we were rich, but it doesn't belong to us. Frankly, I don't know what we should do with it, Lou," his voice quivered. "Someone must know this is here, and eventually they're going to come looking for it. Mrs. Caldwell doesn't know anything about this because if she did, she wouldn't have rented this place to us," he continued while holding his chin with his hand quite bewildered.

Tilting her head, as if a bright light went on, Louise announced, "I bet I know who does know about this treasure, and they live upstairs on the second floor. They may not know exactly where it is, but they know it's here somewhere."

"What are you saying Lou? You think those men are here to steal this?"

"Yes, most definitely Dennis! What are we going to do?"

"You can't be certain about them."

"Yes I can! They were too interested in this place!" she said, adamant in her reply.

"I don't know, Lou. These bars were probably shipped in those crates we have upstairs, but why are they still here?" he asked in search of an answer.

All morning they speculated what they should do. Since the bars had Spanish inscriptions on them, they assumed the bounty was acquired illegally, originating from Mexico most likely, but with a small probability of it originating from Spain.

"I don't understand why this wasn't discovered before now," pondered Louise.

"We didn't discover the wood on the floor was loose even after walking on it, sweeping and mopping it. If I hadn't been searching for entryways for mice, I wouldn't have found it when I did," said Dennis.

"What do you mean?"

"All four of your traps were full this morning."

"Oh yuck!"

"The likelihood that the treasure would have been discovered was slim and whoever planted it in the cellar knew that it was cleverly hidden."

"Why hasn't the owner come forth and claimed it?" asked Louise.

"Maybe the person is dead. There is no telling how long the bars have been hidden here, but I'd speculate that it has been here over forty years," contemplated Dennis. "I'm basing my theory on the metal and design of the candlestick holders on the wall and the way the concrete was applied to the walls."

"Mrs. Caldwell might know who previously owned this place."

"We can't approach her outright without her becoming suspicious. This is her property and if no one claims this treasure she would be entitled to it," warned Dennis.

"Even though you found it?"

"Yes, Lou, by right it would belong to her, at least in Texas that's how it works. I can't see California being any different."

"Dennis, we'll be away from the house during the day, what will stop those men from breaking into our home?"

Considering their options, he said, "I can nail down the windows so that they can only be lifted so high but that won't stop them from breaking the glass and coming in. I can put more support around the doorframe so that if anyone tries to break in, they will have to use an extreme amount of force and the noise might alert Mrs. Caldwell or some of the other neighbors."

"I'm scared. Perhaps we should call Henry and ask him for advice."

"No. I don't want him to get involved in this. It may be dangerous."

Louise shuddered with fear.

"Dennis, the crates are a dead giveaway that the treasure is in close proximity or was at least here at one time."

"I know. We better get rid of them. After I patch up the holes the mice have been using down there and we put out poison, you can help me carry the crates down below."

"After all the washing and sorting I've done with them. Now I have to dismantle my living room and empty all your tools and the other objects out of them," she brooded.

Assiduously, they moved the crates until all of them were coveted away. Dennis was not convinced that the new tenants were there to steal the treasure, because there was not enough proof, but he felt caution was required. The idea occurred to him to build a shed with the leftover plywood in the yard to house the miscellaneous items in their backyard and in the second bedroom. There was not enough wood to complete the project, but he could at least start it. After assembling the frame for it, he placed nails for Louise to hammer in. Utilizing her hammering as a diversion, Dennis went inside the house to hammer nails into the loose floorboard sealing the treasure up completely. Once he finished, he quickly joined Louise outside and continued working on the shed.

Within minutes of their hammering, Mark and Paul appeared causing Louise to wrench, which clearly demonstrated to them that their presence startled her. The two men approached with friendly greetings and asked if they could be of assistance. Dennis declined their help and kept on working. Excusing herself, Louise nervously entered the house. She watched the men from the living room windows and their sudden appearance confirmed her suspicion of them. She went in the backroom and rearranged things by placing them over the secret door to camouflage it.

Sporadically going to the windows to check on Dennis' progress, she saw that he allowed the men to help him construct the shed. Fighting down thunderous bile, she would not dare venture outside to protest. When her eyes met Mark's, he presented her with a surreptitious grin. Grimacing in disgust, she quickly untied the curtains so he could not see inside the house. The men produced beers, and they held a congenial chat while they worked. To distract her mind from perpetrating mayhem on them, Louise turned on the radio and ironed her clothes for work.

Finally, Dennis came into the house bearing a makeshift grin. Controlling her temperament, Louise waited for him to tell her what had transpired.

"Lou, they seem alright. They asked me questions about where we came from, and how we liked it here so far. When I questioned them, they seemed to be two regular guys. They have seen and done a lot because of all of the traveling they have done on their railroad jobs."

"Just what kind of work do they do?" she wanted to know.

"I'm not clear on that. Mark, the son, said that they repair railroad ties and tracks. Paul said they were train inspectors. He explained that they report where repairs need to be made. Maybe they do both. I don't know. When I asked if there was a Mrs. Paul Nielsen, Paul said she left him for another guy years ago. Mark blurted out she died, but Paul promptly corrected him and Mark said he was referring to his own wife."

"How did she die?" Louise asked curiously.

"He never got around to explaining that. We built the shed as far as we could go before running out of wood. Paul was curious as to why we decided to build the shed in that particular spot, but I told him it was the most logical place for it."

"Did they ask you anything unusual?"

"Yeah, they asked me just that; whether we had noticed anything unusual."

"What was your response?"

"I told them there were lots of mice and we laughed."

"They were fishing for information," she concluded. "I bet they've already questioned Mrs. Caldwell," Louise added.

"I don't know Lou. I think you're making a big deal out of nothing."

"I'm going to talk to Mrs. Caldwell and tell her that we noticed someone snooping around in the yard."

"Okay, do what you feel is best."

"Oh Dennis, those men might try to hurt her and us too for that matter."

"Lou, I think you're making a mountain out of a molehill. I wish you would stop! You don't know for sure if they are even after the treasure."

Louise was certain that was their intention, but chose not to debate the issue any further with Dennis. "If you insist, go on and talk to Mrs. Caldwell. Would you ask her, if she wouldn't mind if we gave out her telephone number for emergency purposes, just until we can get our own phone? While you are visiting with her I'm going to reinforce the doorframe," he added.

12

Louise headed for Mrs. Caldwell's front door, but before she could climb the stairs, Mark met her at the foot of the stairs. Cringing at the sight of him, she backed away. He wore a two-piece light brown walking suit and his hair was slicked back on his head dripping from too much gel.

She said, "Hello. Thanks for helping my husband with the shed."

"No problem, anytime. I was hoping you were *gonna* stick around out back and join us for some beers. *Haennnnn!*"

"No, I had other things to do. Excuse me. I'm on my way to see Mrs. Caldwell."

She tried shifting around him, but he counter-reacted, blocking her path. Holding her head high in a regal pose, she stepped backward to maintain a safe distance. Fervently glaring up at him, she did not attempt to conceal her repugnance toward him. His breath reeked from drinking too many beers and smoking cigarettes. Her loveliness captivated him.

"Don't rush off. I'd like to talk to you. *Haennnnn!*"

"I don't think you and I have anything to talk about, mister!"

He raised his hands in a motion that suggested he was about to place them on her waist, but the indomitable way Louise stared at him made him reconsider. Excitement stirred within him as he prepared himself for her to curse or shout at him.

"If you'll excuse me, I have something else to do," she spewed out acidly. In order to pass him she tried to fool him by rushing in the opposite direction, but he quickly jumped in front of her causing his knee to accidentally rise up and rub against her inner thigh.

She cursed and hissed at him, "If you ever touch me again or get in my way you'll be sorry!"

"What are you going to do?" He toyed with her in his cat and mouse game. "Are you *gonna* tell your old man that I rubbed your leg. *Haennnnn!* Come on now, it was an accident. *Haennnnn!*" he taunted her.

The way she gawked at him, coupled with her movements made him grin. Her contemptuous hostility toward him turned him on. Unhurriedly moving aside, he allowed her to climb the stairs.

Calming her unsettled temperament, Louise watched Mark leave the yard and walk down the street. She was still cursing under her breath by the time Mrs. Caldwell answered the door.

"Good evening, dear. Is something wrong?" inquired Mrs. Caldwell after seeing her facial expression.

Louise responded, "I stumbled up the stairs and stubbed my toe, that's all."

)0(

This was the first time Louise was actually inside Mrs. Caldwell's house. Mrs. Caldwell led her into a deep rose-colored living room that led into the dining room. The windows were decorated with lavish cranberry brocade draperies with golden tassels. Near the front windows were matching armchairs, separated by a tiger paw's round mahogany table. A mahogany cocktail table sat between an overstuffed sofa and settee, which were covered with the same fabric as the draperies with delicate embroidered beige lace on the armrests. On each side of the sofa were end tables. On them sat large potbelly lamps made of porcelain with wrought iron overlays with ivory scalloped fringed shades. Finely crafted woodwork surrounded the windows and doorframes giving the room an air of exquisite elegance. Patterns of dark red roses were weaved into an earth tone carpet with shades of beige and brown, which also extended into the dining area. The dining room table seated eight people and a hutch stood against one wall, displaying her fine china. On the credenza was a silver candelabrum with virgin white candles and a pewter vase filled with a bouquet of multi-colored flowers that Louise recognized from Mrs. Caldwell's garden. An ornate brass chandelier, which seemed too grand for the room, hovered over the table.

The older woman offered her something to drink, but she declined and walked around her living room admiring her pictures. Mrs. Caldwell proudly revealed who the people were and explained that she had three children, two daughters and a son. She also expressed that her children and grandchildren lived in Portland and Seattle, and they visited her a few times a year.

"Mrs. Caldwell, as you know, I start work tomorrow, and no one will be at home during the day. I'm afraid since we've painted the coach house it looks more appealing and has drawn the attention of onlookers. I caught a man in the yard earlier today," she lied. "Would you mind keeping your eyes and ears open for any troublemakers?" asked Louise.

"Oh sure, child, you know I didn't think of that. We haven't had any break-ins in this neighborhood, at least, not to my knowledge. I'll keep a look out though. I'm sure you don't have anything to worry about, whoever was in the yard was probably curious about what we've done."

"Thanks Mrs. Caldwell. There's one more favor I'd like to ask. May we use your telephone number as an emergency number, if our family needs to contact us, just until we can afford to get our own phone?"

"Of course, child, I'll write the number down for you."

It was getting dark so Mrs. Caldwell watched Louise walk around the house. "Good luck on your first day at Mr. Hirsch's!" she shouted.

"Thanks, ma'am!"

Cautiously, Louise veered toward her house hoping not to have another encounter with the weasel. *He wouldn't be that bold.* Deliberating against telling Dennis what transpired between them, she felt it wise not to rile him. Their family was not around to support them, and she did not want him to get into any kind of trouble.

)0(

"Did you have a nice visit with Mrs. Caldwell?" asked Dennis.

"I sure did. Her furniture looks like it belongs in a palace somewhere! I only saw the living room and dining room though. She's proud of her children and grandchildren. She has pictures of her family and friends throughout her living room."

Instead of facing him as she spoke, she turned slightly to the side to conceal her discernible disposition.

"Dennis, honey, under the circumstances I think we need to keep something nearby for protection."

"I have my twelve gauge shotgun. I'll keep it loaded and place it on the top shelf in the kitchen pantry."

Turning to face him, demurely, she asked, "Do you have a knife I can carry in my pocketbook?"

Concertedly, Dennis searched her face before settling upon her eyes to see if she would reveal anymore to him, but when she did not elaborate, he replied, "Sure Lou, I'll get it for you."

Sighing with relief that he did not question her further, she looked out of one of the kitchen windows toward the back of Mrs. Caldwell's house. Her attention was directed toward the second floor window where she thought she noticed a quick movement of a curtain. Just as swiftly, she pulled her curtains closed and withdrew from the windows.

That night Louise slept fitfully. Her tossing and turning disturbed Dennis, and he woke her up.

"Lou, are you having a bad dream? Do you feel alright?" he inquired with deep trepidation.

Drowsily, she replied, "Dennis, I'm fine. I'm just jittery about starting my new job."

Formidably, she lied because she did not want to upset him. Concerned for Louise's well being, Dennis pulled his wife toward him, embracing her. Finally, in the safety and comfort of his arms she fell into a serene slumber.

13

The sound of the buzzer from the alarm clock startled Louise when it went off. Looking around, she could not believe that she slept through her husband's departure. Dennis never needed the assistance of a clock to wake him. He could make up in his mind what time he needed to rise and an inner clock would arouse him. Conversely, Louise required the aid of an alarm clock to wake up by, which Dennis set for her before he departed for work. She presumed he decided not to disturb her since she experienced difficulty sleeping during the night. As Louise stirred, she smelled bacon and found a covered plate filled with food on the stove that he left for her. His thoughtfulness pleased her, but she felt guilty for not getting up and preparing his breakfast and lunch.

Gut-wrenching thoughts gnawed at her because she was certain Paul and Mark were there to steal the treasure. She made the decision to take control of her emotions by not allowing this predicament to interfere with the harmony between her and her husband. Comfort was found in her knowing that if the men broke into their home, they would have trouble locating the bullion since it was safely tucked away, and especially if they did not know where to look. As the self appointed guardians of the treasure, it was her and Dennis' responsibility to protect it. What she did not need, however, was the added irritation of the weasel harassing her.

)0(

Louise arrived at Hirsch's Fabrics before Mr. Hirsch and waited patiently in front of the store for him. Moments later a tall bony figure with thinning white hair exited hurriedly from a Ford sedan. Recognizing him as he approached the door, Louise ascertained that he was too pale for her taste and his body seemed to lack muscle tone. Consequently, she presumed the majority of his time was spent indoors working in his shop.

"Good morning, young lady, I must apologize for having you stand outside waiting for me," he said.

"Good morning, Mr. Hirsch, no need to apologize. I haven't been waiting long."

"My wife is recuperating from a recent heart attack. I must assist her in the mornings before leaving for work. A neighbor of ours checks on her throughout the day."

Louise's first day of real employment, as she referred to it, was exciting. She learned how to price each bolt of material and familiarized herself with most of the notions. She cut yards of fabric and ribbons, and before she realized it, the workday was over. The customers appreciated her presence and she enjoyed what she was doing. Mr. Hirsch was sincerely pleased with her performance and by the week's end, he complimented her on how fast she caught on.

Each day she learned new aspects of her job. When new shipments arrived, she checked each item against the invoice and learned how to mark them up for profit. She priced and tagged the notions and procured orders for new merchandise. By the conclusion of the third week, she was efficiently working on her own. Mr. Hirsch felt comfortable enough to give her a key so that she could open and close the store. They coordinated their lunch schedules and she received an hour for lunch. Every so often, she rushed home for lunch, partially checking to see if everything was okay, but oftentimes, she ran errands. Although the store was busiest on Saturdays, she arranged to come in a half an hour later so that she and Dennis could do their grocery shopping together. During this time, they never saw the two men that lived on the second floor. Mrs. Caldwell commented that they must have been out of town working because there was no evidence of their presence.

After a month passed, Louise sold her first sewing machine to a customer who received a discount because she traded in her old machine. Mr. Hirsch cleaned it up, oiled it, and was prepared to resell it, when Louise approached him for it. Prepayment arrangements were made for him to take weekly deductions from her pay, until it was paid for.

)0(

On an impulse one afternoon, Louise ventured into the second hand store on the next block and found two matching end tables which were badly scarred and a couple of old lamps. After negotiating a decent price for the items, she paid for them and told the salesman that her husband would pick them up. When Dennis took her to work on the following Saturday, he picked up the sewing machine and the furniture. The sewing machine was placed in the extra room where Louise planned to undertake several projects in her spare time. After Dennis sanded, stained, and varnished the tables, they looked brand new. Louise took on the chore of cleaning the lamps and making new shades for them. Quite pleased with the result, she placed them on the new end tables.

During the weekends, Dennis performed odd jobs for Mrs. Caldwell, including repairing the railing to the banister leading up her front stairs. Since Louise did not have the opportunity to plow out a section of their backyard for her garden, he took the task on, surprising her when she came home from work one Saturday. She did not waste any time in planting meticulously neat rows of tomatoes, beans, and peppers on the side of the yard opposite the apple tree.

)0(

Louise's birthday was coming up. As a gift for her, Dennis was making a table to sit in front of the couch. In a pile of rubble at his job's construction site, he found the remains of an oddly shaped tree trunk with unique looking roots. Stripping it of its bark, he hollowed out some of it and leveled a flat surface down inside it. Subsequent to sanding and varnishing the table, he painted a picture of a field with grass, flowers, and a picnic basket filled with food next to a yellow patch quilted blanket. He glued in miniature trees before finally placing figurines of a couple inside the table. From the hardware store, Dennis ordered a thick piece of circular glass that was carefully scored around the edges to prevent cuts. The circumference of the glass was much wider than the tree trunk and it fit perfectly level across the top of the table. With the consent of Mrs. Caldwell, he wrapped it and hid it in the crawl space underneath her house until he could present it to Louise.

The young couple opened a savings account and arranged to have a telephone. Since Mrs. Caldwell was home during the day, she let the telephone company in their house for the installation. During the week, their evenings were spent together in the living room reading books or newspapers while listening to the radio. Occasionally, Louise spent time sewing in the backroom.

In one of their conversations, they expressed saving enough money to buy a television. At lunchtime Dennis and a few of his co-workers would walk across the street and window-shop, often buying sodas, cigarettes, or browsing in the shops. Albeit the men were somewhat grubby in appearance from working, the shop owners did not mind because they knew where they worked and welcomed their money.

On lunch one day, Dennis accompanied a co-worker to a furniture store so he could make a payment on the bedroom set he purchased on credit. The electronic section caught Dennis' attention and he moseyed over to examine the television and Hi-fi stereo sets. Succinctly, a friendly, fast talking salesman approached him.

"Look at the quality of the picture," said the salesman. "Let's check out the sound of this record." He played *Ain't Nobody's Business If I Do*, a song from a Billie Holiday album. "Let's add some bass," he suggested bending over to make the adjustment. Bobbing his head up and down to the music, Dennis was hooked. The salesman honed in for the kill, "Feel the quality of the woodwork, only RCA puts all this craftsmanship into one package, my man. It's yours for only a few bucks a month." Bong! The deal was sealed. He convinced Dennis to purchase the brand new combination television/Hi-fi unit on credit. All he had to do was complete the credit application. Dennis went back the following day, made a deposit on it, and was able to pick up his new TV/Hi-fi set after work.

That evening he burst into the house shouting ecstatically, "Hey Lou, I need your help carrying something into the house!"

"Hi, hon. Can it wait a few minutes? I can't leave the stove right now."

He went back out to the truck to let the backdoor down and anxiously waited for her to help him. Removing her apron and placing it on a chair, Louise headed for the door. Not knowing what to expect, she walked through the back gate to the truck and saw Dennis standing next to a large cardboard box that read, "RCA television/Hi-fi combo." Frozen in place Louise looked on in astonishment.

"Well, are you just going to stand there with your mouth gaped wide open? Can I get some help with this?" he asked impatiently.

"Dennis, where did you get this?"

"From a store across the street from where I work."

"Can we afford this?"

"Yeah, Lou!"

"Are you sure?"

"Yes, Lou!" he replied. "I paid a fourth down and will make monthly payments until it's paid for. Are you *gonna* continue just standing there *yappin'* or are you *gonna* help me get this into the house?"

Their evening was spent checking out the different television stations, playing the radio, and listening to the Billie Holiday album the salesman had thrown in for free.

)0(

After breakfast one particular morning, Louise felt nauseated and had to rush to the bathroom. Assessing that she ate something that had upset her stomach, she soon realized after several mornings of this repetitive act, she missed her menses. In the afternoon, she walked over to Dr. Smelling's office and made an appointment for the following day. Louise received confirmation that she was six weeks pregnant. Recounting the days, she knew exactly when she conceived; it occurred on their journey from Texas during their nightly camp stops. *So this is the cause of the unexplainable fatigue I've been experiencing,* she contemplated. With a feeling of jubilation, she placed her hands upon her belly and imagined how she would look in the maternity clothes she would make.

It was Tammy and Henry's week to host dinner and they planned a birthday celebration for her, *But not this week,* she deliberated. Desiring a private celebration between her and her husband, she planned a candlelight dinner. *As if we haven't had enough of candlelights,* she chuckled. Louise bought a roast to prepare for Saturday's meal and decided to wear the blue chiffon gown she was making. She called Tammy, informed her of the news, and swore her to secrecy, until she could tell Dennis.

"I guess this means your birthday party will have to wait until next weekend," mocked Tammy.

14

Ironically, Paul and Mark did work for the Pacific-Atlantic Railroad. They assisted with loading and unloading the freight, and traveling with the train to aid with receiving new shipments along the way. Upon the train reaching its final destination, they cleaned the chemical or substance spills, cattle, and other animal excrements.

Paul Nielsen was a professional thief and con artist that preyed mostly on women. He schooled himself by reading books on the workings of the mind and could have pursued a flourishing career in psychology. Instead, he chose to use this knowledge to manipulate people, an avenue that suited his personality well. With no desire to work hard as a young man, he found satisfactory employment in the restaurant industry, especially ones that served exquisite cuisine. Ostentatiously working as a maitre d', he learned to influence his customers by suggesting the most expensive meals. In return, he received generous tips for his superb service and advice. The restaurant owners were more than satisfied with his performance because the customers he served paid the most money.

In addition to his quality service, he inconspicuously flirted with the female patrons by resting his hand on the back of their chairs. He used his fingers to play with a shoulder or back. Often he would pick up a napkin that might have fallen from a female patron's lap, which he graciously retrieved and replaced on their laps, but with a slight of hand, he brushed against a leg or thigh.

The debonair air in which he presented himself drew the attention of the women patrons who viewed him as profoundly handsome. To most of them, his outlandish conduct was captivating. The ones that took offense accepted his gracious apology for the accidental act, but the need to apologize was very rare.

Many female patrons that were pleased with his charismatic conduct returned to the restaurants without their male companions, often accompanied by female associates, insisting upon being seated at a table that would be served by him. Arrangements were made between them and they would meet on a secret rendezvous, where Paul would provide sexual favors for one or two women at a time. They lavished him with gifts of money and expensive trinkets. This attributed to his inflated ego, increasing his ability to take advantage of their generosity. For example, if one of them wrote a check to him for $50.00 he fraudulently changed the amount and cashed it for $500.00. When the women caught up with him for his wrongdoings, he worked them out by becoming their sexual or licentious servant until the debt was paid.

Successfully, Paul gave the impression to others that he was very well off. In actuality, he managed to live in moderately priced apartments that he copiously decorated with flawlessly second hand furnishings, to create an alluring and seductive atmosphere for his sex-craved guests in need of privacy. By maintaining used vehicles he obtained from one previous owner or from someone's "*lil' ole*" aunt who hardly ever drove it, and eating food from the restaurants where he worked he socked away his money with the realization that his tomorrows were never guaranteed. He planned each day as if it were his last of freedom. By eavesdropping on his financial customers, he learned to invest in stocks, bonds, and expensive jewelry, all of which helped him to maintain his roguish lifestyle.

He often lied about his background, stating that he came from a well to do family that had fallen upon hard times due to his father losing his company because larger companies pushed him out of business. In actuality, his father was a factory worker and his mother a housekeeper. Up until he was fifteen years old, he accompanied his mother on her job and helped with odd tasks. His mother worked for a well-to-do banker and his wife. When they gave parties, Paul also helped serve food and drinks.

The banker had a daughter Paul's age, and when the girl's mother noticed that her daughter was infatuated with Paul, she sent him away. By this time, Paul had gotten a taste of the finer things that life had to offer and working in a factory like his father was not the answer. He saw himself with a better life. He did not have the money to attend a scholastic institute for higher learning that would provide him with the education he desired. At the age of eighteen, he sought employment at a popular restaurant, where they hired him as a porter. He listened to his co-workers and customers and learned from their experiences. He began studying people and realizing how gullible they were. Since he was too young to hang out with some of his co-workers after work, he utilized his time by reading sociology and psychology books that he obtained from the used book store near the restaurant. That was the beginning of his interest in manipulating people.

)0(

A suspicious husband followed his unsuspecting wife. Allowing her and Paul time to become deeply engrossed in their private activity, he jimmied the lock to the door and entered Paul's apartment. Holding a gun in his hand, the husband stood at the bedroom's entrance watching Paul seduce his wife. Slightly cocking his head to the side, full of curiosity, he gazed upon the state of affairs before him.

Paul noticed the husband first, but also observed his loosened hold on his gun and the intrigue that possessed him because of what Paul was doing to his wife. He rose slowly from his entanglement and when the wife realized her husband was standing over them with a gun, she screamed, reached for the sheet to cover herself, and pleaded for forgiveness. Paul yanked the cover from the woman as she cowered and curled in a tight fetal position wailing. To comfort her, he caressed her but cautiously kept his eyes on her husband. He motioned with one hand for the husband to join him. In a calming tone, the rogue instructed the woman to assist her husband in removing his clothing, while he eased the gun away from him. Chuckling to himself as he manipulated the couple, Paul knew he was in total control of the situation. He ordered the couple to kiss and fondle each other, before he joined in. The woman caught on and promptly serviced the two men without hesitation. This began a weekly occurrence in which Paul was paid handsomely.

Paul's existence in this fashion went on for years until another suspicious husband investigated a check his wife had written to him for $1,000.00. When it was discovered that the check had been altered from $100.00, he ended up spending two years in a penal institution. In prison, he perfected his skills by learning new con games. He spent additional time being incarcerated for finagling thousands of dollars from an older woman who thought he was genuinely assisting her in starting a new business. Squandering his life in and out of the penitentiary, during his freedom, he plotted and executed schemes on his next victims.

Prior to a year ago, he spent two years in prison for committing a felony for check forgery. This was where he met his current companion, Mark, who was serving time for rape, assault, and battery. Although Mark was not a bad looking fellow, he was intolerant to the pursuit and chase game regarding women and considered the whole process boring. He sought more excitement and found pleasure in taking what he wanted.

Upon release from prison, the men got jobs with the railroad company. On one of their trips, they overheard dialogue between two men regarding the missing treasure of gold and silver that was stolen in 1910 from Mexico City. Francisco Madero, an aristocrat, was elected as president of Mexico on a platform of social reform. His reign was short lived because he was clueless when it came to politics. Before being ousted from office, he secreted away hundreds of crates containing gold and silver bullion and stored them on ships with the intention of keeping them for himself. Losing control of his ships, Pedro Castillo, a shrewd sea captain, overtook them. He sailed the ships up the coast of the Pacific Ocean around Baja California in Mexico up to Los Angeles, where the bullion was illegally sold to the highest bidders.

Robert Fitzgerald, a prominent rancher purchased several of the crates of bullion. He sold some of the bounty, but kept and stored the rest on his property. His ranch was in Pasadena but when he came to Los Angeles, he resided in a three-story house with a coach house in the back located on Iroquois and Stewart Streets. After his death in 1946, the bullion was never accounted for and there were no records of him ever selling it. His family still owned the ranch in Pasadena but sold the house in Los Angeles. The rumors were that the bullion was buried somewhere between the two properties.

Paul and Mark had worked near the ranch and whenever they had the chance, they scoped the vast property but were never able to pinpoint a possible location for the assumed buried treasure. The Fitzgerald family had undertaken several excavations on the grounds of their ranch and in the yards of the house in Los Angeles. Finally, they gave up the search, figuring that Fitzgerald had disposed of the precious metals years ago. Entrenched in their belief, Paul and Mark were certain that since Los Angeles was closer to the Pacific Coast it was easier for Fitzgerald to have stored the bullion on the property on Iroquois and Stewart Streets, and that it had somehow been overlooked.

)0(

The two men returned from a trip to the Midwest and were off for the next few days. One of the first things they did was take a walk in the alley, entering the backyard of the coach house. It was during the day when neither Louise nor Dennis were at home. Knowing that the Fitzgerald family had already excavated the yard, they poked around the outskirts of the yard with sticks in hopes of finding some signs of a buried treasure. Their attention was drawn to the newly built shed, when some boys passed through the alley. Having to curtail their activity, they went through the yard approaching the rear of the house, encountering Mrs. Caldwell as she exited her backdoor.

"Good morning Paul and Mark, I didn't know you two were back. When did you arrive?"

Paul immediately responded, "We arrived early this morning and just took out the trash."

"Did you have a good trip?"

"Well, it was work, ma'am, you know how that goes. *Haennnnn!*" Mark informed her.

We're exhausted and we're going to retire, if you'll excuse us," said Paul.

"Sure thing. Get some rest, I'll see you later."

15

Mrs. Caldwell's previous tenants were a married couple in their thirties. They lived in her apartment for a couple of years before mysterious misfortunes began occurring. The wife was robbed, beaten, and raped one evening after she left her job. Someone placed a gunny sack over her head, snatched her off the street, and dragged her into a deserted gangway.

A month later, after leaving a currency exchange, the husband was conned out of his paycheck by a man who claimed he found a wallet full of money, belonging to a longshoreman who just cashed his check at the same currency exchange. The conman convinced the husband that the longshoreman had gone into the tavern across the street and had not discovered that his wallet was missing. Collectively, the two men collaborated and upon the suggestion of the conman, they decided that if they approached the longshoreman, he would gladly give them a reward for returning his wallet with all of his money it in. Counting over $2,000.00 in the wallet, the conman figured they would receive at least $200.00 as a reward. The man suggested as a safety precaution, to show in good faith that no one would try to cheat the other, each of them should put their money in a tied up handkerchief. One of them would hold onto the handkerchief until the reward was collected. Since the man was white, the tenant undoubtedly felt he was trustworthy and went along with the scheme. After the man placed all of his money in a handkerchief, the tenant followed suit. Again, upon the decision of the conman, the tenant was allowed to hold the money in the handkerchief for safekeeping. The man disappeared inside the tavern.

After waiting for what seemed to be an indeterminable length of time, the tenant decided to run home with the stuffed handkerchief. Vigilantly watching his back as he ran, when he reached the inside of his apartment, he tore opened the handkerchief expecting to see all of the money, but what he set his eyes on was a stack of cut up newspaper. Too embarrassed, he could not report the pigeon drop incident to the police or anyone else for that matter. If he had not been encompassed with the greed of trying to get something for nothing, he would have never lost his paycheck.

Subsequently, the wife's incessant edginess made her allege that someone was following her. Her fear inhibited her continuance to work. One night, the husband walked across an alley, and he was accosted by a man wearing a ski mask. At gun point, the tenant was robbed of his wallet with all of his money and personal identification in it. At odd times of the night, the couple received telephone calls. Once they answered the telephone, they only heard the sound of muzzled breathing and then the caller hung up. Finally, they decided to move out of state for their own safety and peace of mind.

The couple moved out of Mrs. Caldwell's apartment on Saturday. Early Sunday morning before she left for church, she received an unconventional visit from Paul and Mark, stating that they were interested in renting the apartment. Initially, she planned on listing the apartment for rent on the following Sunday with her church's weekly announcements. This would allow her a week to clean it up. When she inquired how the men found out about the vacant apartment so quickly, they informed her that the previous tenants told them they were moving. They paid her two weeks in advance and stated that they would not be able to move in until the following week because their jobs required them to travel a lot.

)0(

Perched in a comfortable chair on her front porch, Mrs. Caldwell held her Bible in her lap. She was surprised when the white men approached her regarding the apartment since the neighborhood contained Negroes, American Indians, and Mexicans. With money in their hands, their ethnicity did not matter as long as they paid the rent on time and did not damage her property. It was a kind gesture on the behalf of her former tenants, Maurice and Janice, to recommend her apartment to Paul and Mark.

She hated losing her former tenants, but they became disillusioned with the city after things started going wrong for them. Mrs. Caldwell empathized with Janice when she got raped and she personally counseled her to help her regain her trust in men. Coupled with her rape and robbery and her husband's attack, Mrs. Caldwell understood that it was too much for them to endure.

She considered herself privileged to have found new tenants so quickly. She marveled at her good fortune because she didn't even lose a week's worth of rent. Not only did she have tenants upstairs, but lucked out with additional tenants that moved in the deserted coach house who improved her property as well. Rapidly, she was acquiring a fondness for Louise and Dennis. They made her reminisce about her own youth with Percy, her deceased husband. Auspiciously pleased with herself, she picked up her Bible and continued to read.

)0(

On Saturday afternoon, Paul noticed Mrs. Caldwell working in the yard and immediately sent Mark up to the attic to look for any evidence of the missing bullion. Previously, Mrs. Caldwell had offered them storage space in the attic, therefore, he knew it remained unlocked. All Mark found after snooping around were old appliances, boxes, and numerous bags of junk, to his way of thinking. The floor of the attic was solidly constructed of wood. It appeared to be the original floor with no major signs of repair or alterations. Checking the walls, he tapped on them and listened for hollow sounds behind them. Prudently, he pulled back the corners of the aged wallpaper, which crumbled off into his hands as he inspected behind it in search of the hidden treasure. Like a thief in the night, he eased back down the stairs to report his findings to Paul.

Discussing Mark's lack of evidence, Paul construed, "I wasn't sure, but I didn't think the bullion would be up there because the floor of the attic can't sustain its weight. There's a great possibility that it is in the crawl space under the house. First chance you get, you're going to have to crawl underneath the house and investigate it."

"Why do I have to be the one to go crawling and scrounging around under this house getting dirty? Why can't you do it? I'm always the one who has to take the risks! It's your turn! I'm not going underneath this old ass house!" he bellowed.

"The hell you are! If it wasn't for me, you wouldn't be where you are today! Your butt would still be in jail, twiddling your thumbs, trying to figure out how to get out! I'm the person who taught you how to deal with the guards and become a model prisoner! I've taught you how to run the con game on innocent suckers! I even recommended your ass for the railroad job! Now try and tell me why, when I ask you to do something, you give me a hard time about it?" Paul roared, walking up into Mark's chest.

"But I always have to do the dirty work. Can't you do it sometimes? *Haennnnn!*" Mark asked, passively surrendering by backing away.

"I have done my share of the dirty work and I will do it again! But you're going to be the one searching under this house, when the time comes. Here, take this and go and find yourself a woman and have some fun," Paul said handing him a wad of money.

Looking at the newfound wealth in his hand, Mark beamed because he had spent most of his money and only had a fin in his pocket.

"Can I take the car too?" he asked, as if he was a teenager asking his father for the automobile for the evening.

"Of course, my boy, have yourself a good time tonight, and do try to behave yourself," Paul warned him austerely, issuing him a severe no nonsense gawk because of Mark's insatiable taste for roughness. Paul had other plans for the evening and Mark would have only been in his way.

)0(

Mrs. Caldwell was finishing up her yard work when Paul approached her from behind.

With the finesse of a southern gentleman, exhibiting all of his pearly whites, he said, "Mrs. Caldwell, you have such a lovely garden. Most folks are so busy nowadays that they don't take advantage of spending time doing what they truly enjoy. Looking at your pretty flowers and those neatly planted vegetables, expresses all the tender loving care you have devoted to them. It reminds me of a piece of art. The pleasant fragrance emanating out here is all because a special lady such as yourself has taken the time to create all this beauty." Taking a deep breath as he spoke, Paul extended his arm and with a wave of his hand, he pointed toward her flowers. Naively lapping up his compliments, Mrs. Caldwell blushed and glanced at her garden as if she was seeing it for the first time and could exactly see what Paul was referencing.

"Why thank you Mr. Nielsen, nowadays, not too many people appreciate the beauty of a garden."

"Oh do call me Paul, it sounds less formal. Wouldn't you agree?"

"Of course, and by all means, please call me Flora."

"Flora, is that short for Florence?" he asked with a flirtatious tilt of his head.

She nodded agreeably, blushing again.

"What a lovely name for such an adorable lady."

His sugarcoated words reflected his courteous demeanor. Mrs. Caldwell was so tickled that she began fanning herself with one of her gloves. "Thank you," was all she could muster up to say, as another blush formed upon her face.

Mrs. Caldwell was not interested in a relationship with this man and particularly not with a white man, but just the same, she was flattered by his words.

Gathering her things, she changed the subject. She said, "I'm all finished working out here for today, and it is time for me to prepare my supper."

Endowed with a broad grin Paul said, "And I'm about to do the same. My boy, Mark, is going out for the evening, and I'm going to have a quiet meal at home alone. Would you care to join me?"

"Oh no, I couldn't do that. I already have some meat thawing out on the counter. How about you joining me for supper instead?"

"I'd love to," he answered rather promptly.

"Come down in about an hour and a half then."

16

Dressed in his favorite pair of worn overalls, Dennis used his powerful muscular arms and hands to control the handsaw while cutting plywood in the yard on Saturday. Louise arrived from work hauling a couple of bags from the grocery store. Their lips touched lightly as they greeted hello. Automatically, Dennis took her packages to carry them into the house.

"Did you forget to get something from the store when we went shopping this morning?" he asked as he reached into one of the bags to see what was there.

Slapping his hand out of her bag, she smiled, "No! And stop being so nosey! I needed to get a few more things."

"Ouch! You're a mean woman!" he replied good naturedly. "What time do you want to leave for Tammy and Henry's?"

Her face possessed a mischievous beam. Louise responded, "I called Tammy and told her we weren't coming over this weekend, since it's my birthday tomorrow. I'd rather have a private celebration with just the two of us. I hope you don't mind." She explored his face for approval.

"No, not if that's what you want. I would have liked for you to have a cake or something, Lou." The disappointment could be heard in his voice.

"I have one," she gestured to one of the sacks. "How about you continuing to build more shelves for your shed and come inside later."

"Okay," he agreed harmoniously.

Spending the evening alone with his wife, not sharing her attention with anyone else suited him just fine. Originally, Dennis ruminated giving her the gift he made for her on Sunday, but now was certainly the opportune time. He was confronted with getting the large table passed the kitchen windows without Louise seeing him. While she was busy in the kitchen, he went to retrieve the table from underneath Mrs. Caldwell's house.

After loading the table onto the dolly, he set it off to the side. He raced to a kitchen window and peeped inside. Once he saw Louise head toward the back of the house, he rushed to retrieve the table. The dolly wobbled awkwardly as he hurriedly made his way through the yard. The table ended up slipping off of the dolly and tearing some of the paper used to conceal it, exposing some of its roots. It resembled the tentacles from an octopus. Repositioning the table onto the dolly, his efforts made him sweat profusely. Cautiously studying the window, halfway through the yard, Louise came into his view. He stopped motionless, like a cornered rabbit in a field, hoping to remain undiscovered. Perhaps in his mind, she would not notice the large curious object, which stuck out on both sides that he was trying to smuggle past her view. When Dennis felt it was safe to move, he readjusted his parcel, by turning the dolly around and walking backward. Finally, making his way past the window, he stored the table in a section of their yard out of sight.

)0(

Finishing up with her bath, Louise ran water for her mate before she shouted, "Dennis! Time to come in!" While he bathed, she hurriedly changed into her new dress and lit the candles she set on the kitchen and living room tables.

Upon exiting the bathroom in semidarkness, Dennis saw a glow of light stemming from the front of the house. After dressing in the bedroom in clothes that Louise had laid out for him, he dabbed on some rose water cologne and walked toward the kitchen.

At the entrance of the kitchen, Dennis stood inhaling the vision of his lovely wife's golden brown skin, which glistened underneath the flickering of the candlelights. His eyes were drawn to the low neckline of her blue dress settling upon her full rounded breasts. The rise and fall of her chest as she took each breath aroused him. Her moist lips covered with a touch of red lipstick beckoned him.

He hesitated before saying in a deep husky voice, "Lou, you look gorgeous in that dress. Is it the one you've been working on?"

"Yes, hon. I'm glad you like it. You look pretty smart yourself, mister, in that silk shirt."

Donning a broad grin, Dennis pulled her toward him, smothering her tender lips with his own.

When she tried to pull away, he held her firmly before saying, "Not yet, let me hold you. I'm enjoying the way you look and smell. Notice anything about me?" he asked, raising his chin up in the air.

Sniffing at the side of his face, she said, "Sure do. You put on the rose water cologne without me telling you to."

"Didn't think you'd notice," he smiled, embracing her and deepening his kiss.

Only when he had his fill of her did he release her.

"The table *shore* is set pretty," he commented, as he admired the candles and decorative centerpiece that were sitting on the table. "I suspect the tablecloth, napkins, and fancy napkin holders are newly made by you as well."

Blushing she replied, "Yes, they are. Thanks, sweetheart."

"Lou, I have never been in a real fancy restaurant, but it can't be any better than this." He assisted Louise into her chair.

)0(

Toward the end of their supper, Dennis remarked, "As always, Lou, your meal is splendid. You put your foot in the pot roast, mashed potatoes, and carrots. I consider myself lucky to have a wife who is such a fine cook. You know, there isn't much you don't know how to do."

Louise smiled, as her face reddened.

"Now, is my pretty wife blushing over there? Come here." Pushing himself back from the table, firmly planting his feet on the floor, Dennis gestured for her to join him. Louise flew from her seat to sit on his lap. Enthralled by her eyes, he held her. Pulling her toward him, he smothered her with his kisses.

Finally, urging her up, he led her into the living room where he turned on the Hi-fi set and put on a Cab Calloway album. Louise stood in place watching her husband. The admiration she possessed for him was visible on her face. Her heart fluttered and felt as if it were about to burst from happiness. They slow danced to a few songs before he steered her toward the couch. He planted warm kisses on her eyelids and nose before reaching her yielding lips. Massaging her back with his hand, Dennis found that he could not keep his hands off of her any longer. He lowered one shoulder of her dress. Eagerly, she assisted him in removing her dress and undergarments. The center of the rug in front of the couch became the destined place for their inevitable lovemaking. The soft glow from the candlelights outlined their bodies, displaying their silhouettes upon the wall. Louise purred, "I love you Dennis Clark! I love you so much! You make me feel so good!" That was all he needed to hear before he made his final thrusts between her sweet thighs.

Afterwards, lying in each other's arms, they stared at the stars in the sky through the living room windows. For the longest time, neither of them spoke a word, not wanting to break the alluring spell.

"Lou, I love you, there could never be anyone else for me, but you," Dennis finally said softly.

"Oh sweetheart, don't you know by now we're made for each other?"

"I guess, I do. I have something for you, I need to go and get it."

Quickly putting on his trousers and shoes, Dennis headed for the door. Louise freshened up before replacing her clothing, but remained barefoot. When she returned to the living room, Dennis was sitting on the couch.

He said, "These are for you," extending his arms to hand her a card and a bouquet of flowers.

Louise read the card out loud. *"Happy Birthday to the one I love. This is for the special lady in my life. You and only you are responsible for my happiness. Love, Dennis."* As Louise read the evocative words, she inhaled deeply, overwhelmed by the eternal affection she felt for her mate. With watery eyes, she removed the wrapper from the flowers, gazing upon a combination of peach, yellow, and white tulips mixed with daffodils.

"These are so beautiful!" she said reaching over to hug him.

"You deserve them," he replied returning her embrace. "I'll be right back." Reluctantly, he pulled away from her.

"Where are you going this time?" Quizzically, her eyes followed him as he left out of the house.

Louise remained seated, but stared at the door with the anticipation of a young child waiting for Santa Claus to come. The banging of a door startled her when Dennis reentered struggling to get a large object in the house. She jumped up to help him by holding the door.

Overflowing with cheer, she clapped her hands as she asked, "What in the world is this?"

"Lou, please have a seat on the couch," he responded out of breath.

Doing as she was told, Louise repeated, "Dennis, what is this?" her voice elevated an octave with exhilaration.

"You'll see."

He placed the peculiar shaped object in the center of the rug, where they had just made love. "Open it Lou," he encouraged, standing back to give her some space.

Rising from her seat, she tore away the newspaper and string. Unable to believe her eyes, Louise stood back and looked incredulously at the strangely-shaped object. In order for her to see and appreciate her gift, she pulled the chain to the ceiling light. In awe of his ingenuity, she announced, "Dennis, this is beautiful! You made this?" It was more of a statement than a question. "When did you have time to make this?" With her hands on the glass, she looked down into the table. "Oh, how cute, the couple is having a picnic. You're so creative! I bet no one in the world has a table like this! Thank you sweetheart!" she exclaimed, running her hand over it to examine the wood and admiring his artisanship.

Dennis stood watching his wife feeling warmheartedly proud that he was responsible for her glee. Tightly, she hugged and kissed him.

"If you keep this up, I'm *gonna* have trouble letting you go," he said gazing down into her eyes.

"Promise?" she replied. "I'd like for you to come and have a seat. I have something wonderful to share with you." Focusing on the center of the table, she said, "I really like my gift, but do you see that couple there?" as she pointed her forefinger downward on the glass of the table.

"Yes," he replied, nodding and looking at the miniature figurines of the man and woman in the picnic scene.

"You're going to have to add one more person, a rather small person."

Immobilized, Dennis searched her face for some form of comprehension of what she said, or at least what he thought he heard her say. His piercing stares could have seared her skin. Unable to sit still any longer, he arose from the couch, walked over to the windows and then returned, before replying, "Lou, do you mean that we're going to have a baby?"

"Sure do," she nodded, smiling at his perplexity.

"You're not kidding, are you?"

Shaking her head she replied, "No, sweetheart, I'm not."

"Oh boy, this is the best news I've ever had. I'm going to be a father! When did this happen? How long have you known?"

"I'm six weeks pregnant and I found out this week."

Grinning from ear-to-ear, he said, "Honeybunch, come here." He pulled her toward him in an embrace. "I love you."

"And I love you back."

"This calls for a celebration, where is that birthday cake?"

"You and that stomach of yours," she giggled.

17

While Louise and Dennis were having their celebration, Paul and Mrs. Caldwell met for dinner. Paul arrived at Mrs. Caldwell's house in a dark dinner jacket and freshly creased matching pants. As he passed her, she inhaled a whiff of his pleasant fragrance. "Good evening Flora, whatever you have prepared for dinner smells awfully good." He recognized the aroma of smothered pork chops with onions, but chose not to comment.

"I thought this might go well with our meal," he said, handing her a bottle of chilled rose wine.

"Thank you. This is very thoughtful of you."

Upon entering her house after completing her yard work, Mrs. Caldwell bathed and changed into a floral summer dress. She also touched up her curls, which were flattened underneath the straw hat she always wore when working in the yard.

"Your dress is very pretty."

"Thank you, dear, it is nothing special."

"Ah, I see the lady doesn't wish to accept my compliment graciously."

"Oh, that's not it. Thank you though. You're just having an informal meal with your landlord, that's all."

She wanted to set the record straight because she had qualms regarding inviting him to dinner in the first place.

Sensing her reservations, Paul immediately suggested, "Let's have a glass of wine." His intention was to relieve the awkwardness she felt.

Mrs. Caldwell brought two glasses but experienced difficulty in finding a corkscrew to open the wine bottle. Paul volunteered to go upstairs to his apartment to get one, but she insisted upon finding hers by searching through several kitchen drawers. Behind her back, while she searched, he rolled his eyes and shook his head in repugnance. *I won't have to work hard trying to please her. The fat bitch doesn't even know where her corkscrew is.* Finally, producing it, Paul opened the bottle and gulped down two glasses to help him get through the evening. Their time was spent at the dining room table, discussing their families and friends. Mrs. Caldwell sat at the head of the table with Paul on her right side.

"Whatever happened to your husband?" Paul asked inquisitively. After listening to Mrs. Caldwell's explanation regarding his accident, he replied with remorse, "I'm sorry to hear about your loss. What a tragedy, to have lost your loved one that way. It had to have been wearisome on you, especially with your children living so far away." He reached over, grasped her hand, and lightly patted the back of it to comfort her.

Sharing his own sob story, he explained to her how he spent most of his time on the road. "My wife of fifteen years cheated on me, while I traveled," he declared as his words flowed smoothly out of his mouth. "I didn't find out until I came home from one of my long trips with the railroad. Upon my return home, the house was empty, except for my clothing and a few personal things that I collected throughout the years. She left me for another man and took all the furniture and things we acquired together." The cunning rogue observed her and after receiving the reaction he sought, he continued with his tale of lies. Paul reported to her the saga of being wounded and devoting his time and money to someone who was so ungrateful.

"I went on a path of destruction after that, careless drinking, and floundering around with loose women. I got involved in a nonsense altercation in a bar with another man over the attention we both received from a woman. The other man seethed with jealousy and approached me by picking a fight. Now mind you that I'm not a big man and even though he was much larger than me, I held my own with him. We caused such a disruption that it landed us both in jail overnight. It was a horrifying experience. It was so embarrassing being at the police station and the thought of being locked up behind bars traumatized me to no end." As Paul spoke, he waved his hands in the air and bucked his eyes to accentuate his tale. "You wouldn't believe the mentality of the people I encountered in jail that night. That incident was enough to turn my head around. After that night, I prayed to God and promised myself that I wouldn't do anything else ever to put myself in that kind of predicament. Oh, the thought of it, still sends chills through me." Femininely, he raised his right hand and allowed it to linger in the air as he bent it down at the wrist adding extra emphasizes to his speech.

This time Mrs. Caldwell comforted him by reaching for his hand and holding it. "Paul, that had to be a devastating experience, one that got you back on the right path I see. Praise the Lord! You were one of the lucky ones. You could have lost your job and everything you worked so hard for."

"I know," responded Paul, nodding in agreement.

"I have a friend whose husband left her for a younger woman who couldn't cook and didn't know the first thing about house-keeping. It didn't matter to the husband because he was having too much fun with her sexually and all. He got sick and was ill for a couple of months. Either the young woman didn't want to take care of him or just didn't have *the know how*. She was so wrapped up in herself that she wasn't cooking meals for him either. All she wanted to do was go out to drink, party, and spend his money on clothes for herself. The poor man was losing weight that he really couldn't afford to lose because he needed the nourishment to help him heal."

"He went back to his wife pleading to come home so she could take care of him properly. Initially, she refused but finally gave in because he cried like a baby and swore that he recognized the error of his ways. He learned the valuable lesson that youth and beauty aren't important. He has been back with his wife for several years now, and he is such a devoted God *fearin'* man and dutiful husband," Mrs. Caldwell concluded.

"I can certainly appreciate that, but I would have never put myself in that kind of situation," replied Paul expressing his empathy.

Paul helped Mrs. Caldwell clear away the table. When he insisted upon helping clean up the dishes, she flatly refused. She offered him some whiskey and they adjourned to the living room.

"Since your wife left you, it was commendable for you to stay in contact with your son. Many men don't do that," said Mrs. Caldwell, facing Paul while sitting on one end of the sofa.

"Huh?" he uttered.

Rephrasing her statement, she said, "Even though your wife left you, you maintained a nice lasting relationship with your son, since you are working and living together."

"Oh yeah," he responded quickly, cognitive of making a perfunctory mistake.

Paul left after a few hours and found that not only had he enjoyed the meal, but also enjoyed her company. Sniggering as he thought about it, he brought wine to dinner, but found out that Mrs. Caldwell was a whiskey drinker. She could definitely hold her liquor well. More importantly, he was able to leave her apartment with a good conception of how it was set up. He would need this information later when he would return to search her place for the missing bullion.

18

Sunday morning after Mrs. Caldwell left for church, Paul went down the back stairs to see if he could get into her apartment. Finding the doors and windows tightly secured, he walked around the outside of the house, inspecting the front inside door and the remaining windows. Encountering neighbors on each side of the house, he had to forego his inspection. The neighbors were black and when he attempted to exchange greetings with them with a wave of his hand, they responded by spying on him with curious stares.

Without the proper tools to jimmy the locks to Mrs. Caldwell's front and backdoors, entry was impossible. Paul resolved that he would obtain the tools from a hardware store. Breaking and entering was not his forte, but after spending time being incarcerated, through the invaluable education of the penal system, he received explicit instructions from his fellow inmates. He would be traveling on the road in a few days, therefore, it would be weeks before his next opportunity to get inside her apartment.

Loud throaty snores evolved from Mark's bedroom, greeted Paul when he entered his apartment. Mark had a late night of carousing and returned home early in the morning. Recounting the events from the previous evening, Paul made a note to buy a bottle of Mrs. Caldwell's favorite whiskey, construing that he'd have to hide it to keep Mark from drinking it. Paul needed to peruse Dennis and Louise's backyard more closely, and when possible, gain access inside their house while they were at work. Things were progressing as planned. Being a patient man, he postulated that he had plenty of time on his hands.

)0(

Mrs. Caldwell arose from her slumber reflecting on the past evening, accepting it as a pleasurable one. She considered herself fortunate for having such an agreeable man as a tenant. Witty and entertaining in his conversation, characteristically, she also found him to be thoughtful and kind. Gathering her things, she prepared for a long day at church, filled with ushering people to their seats, singing, rejoicing, and praising the Lord.

Her grandchildren were coming to visit and stay with her during their summer vacation. She was excited about having her home filled with their cheer and laughter. In preparation of their visit, she needed to clean up the attic so it could be utilized as extra living space. Although stairs led to the attic from the second floor landing, she wanted access to the attic from her kitchen, and the current door to the attic needed a lock installed. Mrs. Caldwell wondered if Dennis would have time to construct a portion of the attic into two bedrooms and a recreational area. Deacon Reid, a semi-retired plumber who was rather sweet on her, told her that he could install plumbing for the bathroom, whenever she was ready. She had already mapped out the place for it, and he promised to come by after church to look at it.

)0(

Deacon Reid and Mrs. Caldwell pulled up in his car as Mark and Paul were leaving out of the house. Their departure surprised Deacon Reid because he had no idea that they were living upstairs. Immediately, he became defensive.

Not shy of standing up for himself even in the presence of white folks, loudly he announced, "Hey, what are you two doing here?" His tone was brusque, as if he were the proprietor with authority.

The two men were somewhat thrown off guard. Paul replied obnoxiously, "We live here buddy, now if you don't mind."

Paul and Mark were trying to open the gate to leave, but Deacon Reid stood with his shoulder squared, defiantly blocking their exit. Mrs. Caldwell, realizing the situation was rather unnerving, intervened by placing her hand on one of his arms.

She announced, "Deacon Reid, I would like for you to meet my new tenants, Paul Nielsen and his son, Mark."

"Oh, howdy," he replied easing his guard only slightly, "I didn't know you had them for new tenants."

Succinctly turning toward Mrs. Caldwell, he flexed his body, but remained in place blocking the gate.

He asked, "When did they move in?"

"They moved in a few weeks ago, I thought I mentioned that to you, last time you were here."

"Maybe you did, but omitted to tell me they were ah…I don't remember," he replied, displaying his disapproval of the men by surveying them from head to toe, through his thick glasses and upturned nose, as if they stunk. With his face contorted in a frown, he moved aside, allowing the men to leave the yard.

Begrudgingly, Paul was taken aback by this encounter. It was annoying, because he did not need any additional interference with his plans.

"We were just leaving to go out to supper. Would you care to join us?" Paul asked out of courtesy, but wholeheartedly did not mean it.

"No thanks! We ate supper at church," replied Deacon Reid matching Paul's despicable tone.

Mrs. Caldwell attempted to alleviate the tension by saying, "Have a good evening, I'll see you later."

Deacon Reid followed her up the stairs, but he stood at the top of the stairs watching the men get in their car to leave.

Grilling her with questions, he asked, "Who are they? How did they found out about your apartment?"

"They are two nice men who work for the Pacific-Atlantic Railroad. Their time is spent mostly traveling with the trains."

"What do they do for the railroad?"

"I believe that they are inspectors and report if there is any damage to the tracks and freight cars."

"*Humpf!*" he uttered cynically.

"What does *humpf* mean?" she asked, shaking her head to his indifference.

"They look like jailbirds to me, I can spot them a mile away."

"Rufus, how dare you say such a mean thing?" she huffed.

"I'm not being mean Flora, but those men have spent time in jail. They're up to something. Why are they living here in this neighborhood? Look around you woman! No whites live here, and why would they want to live among us?" he forcefully inquired. "Doesn't that seem a little odd to you?"

"I never gave it much thought."

"Well I suggest that you do!" he continued to growl. "When did they move in?" he reiterated.

"About four or five weeks ago."

"Four or five weeks ago! Why didn't you tell me?"

"I did! You must not have paid any attention to what I said."

"Flora, you know *dag gone well* that you didn't tell me you have two white men living upstairs from you!"

Mrs. Caldwell fiddled with her hair.

"How did they know that you had a vacancy?"

Trying to recall what had transpired between her and the two men, she walked over to the settee in the living room and sat down. Deacon Reid followed her, removing his suit jacket and loosening his tie.

"Oh yeah, I remember, they said that Maurice and Janice, my previous tenants, told them they were moving out."

"Did you confirm this with them?"

"No, because they had moved already. How else would they have known about my apartment?" I hadn't mentioned it to anyone else yet.

"*Humm,*" he said.

Exasperated by his comments, Mrs. Caldwell began to grit her teeth. After all, it was her house and her property. He did not have any say so in her affairs. He was a friend, a good friend, who had been by her side for several years. Their relationship was a comfortable one and sometimes she requested his assistance with her decision-making. When her children and their families were in town, he was always included in their gatherings and they readily accepted him. Demurely, she never considered him other than an admirable friend; it wasn't that he hadn't tried to be more. She had a house and was not going to let some man profit from the things she earned by herself.

Deacon Reid confessed that he had been married but did not have any children that he was aware of. He worked for years as a plumber and now resided in a retirement complex. In his retirement, he took on occasional plumbing jobs. Although he was a good companion to Mrs. Caldwell, he was not ambitious enough for her. Yearly, he traveled to Georgia to visit a younger brother who lived there. Other than that, he was content with his life the way it was. When Mrs. Caldwell tried to get him to accompany her when she visited her children, he always came up with flimsy excuses.

Considering the circumstances, that did not give him the right to control her life or put in his two cents where they were not needed.

"Now Rufus, if I feel that I'm in a situation that I can't handle, you would be the first person I'd come to, you know that. I resent you placing my tenants in a negative light," she said. Her annoyance with his remarks was evident by the resonance of her trembling voice.

"But Flora, listen to me! I know those men are bad and have some obscure reason for being here. I don't know how to prove it to you, but if I have to, I'm *gonna!*"

"That's up to you, but don't think you're going to come over here and be rude! Do you understand?" she said with a firm conviction of not taking any further nonsense from him.

"Okay, I'll back off. Did Maurice and Janice leave a phone number where they can be reached?"

Staring him down, she said, "Yes, they did. Didn't I just tell you nicely to mind your own business?"

"Okay, but Flora…."

Mrs. Caldwell interrupted him, taking a deep breath, raising her hand, waving it in the air she said, "It's none of your business! Now leave it alone!"

Determined not to aggravate her anymore, he changed the subject. "How about that dessert you promised me?" he asked.

They adjourned to the kitchen where she put on a pot of coffee before scooping up a couple of bowls of peach cobbler. Their conversation turned to the events of the day.

Deacon Reid's decision to back off from pursuing the conversation about the two men was only temporary. Unwavering in his assumption regarding the men, he decided to use another approach with Mrs. Caldwell to find out more about them. First, he needed to acquire the telephone number of her former tenants. He knew she listed all of her contacts in her address book. He watched her plenty of times as she made new entries and referenced it. Her address book was on the table in her bedroom and somehow he had to get it. Every time he tried to approach Mrs. Caldwell in an amorous manner, she coiled away from him. But tonight was going to be different.

"Have you talked to the carpenter about building the bathroom in the attic?" he asked.

"Well, not yet, but I can call him."

Mrs. Caldwell called Dennis and asked if he could come over to look at the attic regarding a new project she had in mind. Meeting Dennis at her backdoor, she said, "Thanks for coming over so quickly, Dennis." Introducing the two men, they exchanged handshakes and followed her to the attic. "I would like to know if you would build stairs leading up here from my kitchen and install a few rooms so I can use them for my guests," she asked.

Dennis surveyed the area and converged on a plan. He drafted plans for the stairs, two bedrooms, a moderate sized recreation room, and a full size bathroom, after collaborating with Deacon Reid. "See, here," said Dennis showing her his rough drafts, "there'll be plenty of room left for storage space." After discussing their plans, Dennis asked, "Ma'am, how soon did you want me to start the job? I can devote my weekends to it and maybe some evenings if I'm not too tired. I figure we can have this done within a couple of months or less."

"I'm free most of the time," said Deacon Reid. "I can help you whenever you want to work."

"Good deal," said Dennis.

Deacon Reid took an immediate predilection toward Dennis and told him so.

"How much do think it will cost me?" asked Mrs. Caldwell.

"We'll work that out later, after I get prices on the material," said Dennis.

The men exchanged telephone numbers before Dennis returned home.

"Nice young man," commented Deacon Reid.

"I told you my new tenants were nice. Wait until you meet Louise, his wife."

"Yep, you did. You just forgot to tell me about the 'other two tenants,'" placing long drawn out emphasis on the words "other two tenants."

"Oh Rufus, hush!"

"I'm thirsty, what have you got to drink?" he asked.

"I can make some iced tea or lemonade."

"No, I'd like something stronger."

"I'm all out of whiskey."

"How can you be all out? I bought you a fifth last week."

With no desire to explain what happened to it, she said formidably, "Daisy and Sarah came over and we had a few drinks."

"Okay, I'll go buy us another one, I'll be right back," he said, as he grabbed his Stetson hat and tweed jacket before leaving out of the front door.

Deacon Reid traveled four blocks to the liquor store. There was very little traffic on the street because people had deserted it, returning to their homes to prepare for the beginning of the week. Preoccupied with his course of action for the evening, he parked his car on the corner and hurried into the liquor store three doors away.

19

A couple of hours later Mrs. Caldwell called Deacon Reid at home to see why he changed his mind about returning to her house. Presuming he was upset with her regarding their argument over Paul and Mark, she prepared herself for another confrontation over the telephone. When she did not get an answer, she began to worry. She called a friend that lived in the retirement building to ask him to check on Deacon Reid. He promised to call her back. Agonizing over his whereabouts, she paced and circled the house impatiently. Constantly, she went to the windows to watch for him, anticipating his arrival at any moment.

Torment ridden, she fathomed him in a car accident or having a heart attack. He should not have had a heart attack, because his heart was healthy per his last check up. Perhaps he stumbled and hurt himself. If he had fallen, surely someone saw him and came to his rescue. Was he in a hospital somewhere? Even if he was angry with her, he should have contacted her to let her know what was going on in that thick skull of his. How could he allow her to be tormented like this? Hadn't she made it painstakingly clear that she cared about him? These unanswered questions beleaguered her. She felt guilty about their argument over her "other new tenants." But wasn't she justifiably correct? He had no right to assume the worst about the men. He was simply being unreasonable and she was glad she told him so, but why did she feel so darn guilty? *Rufus Reid, where are you? Where in tarnation are you?*

Not knowing where he was or how he was doing, she went out onto her front porch and stared into the darkness, wondering. Infrequently when a car drove by, she stared at it, hoping it was Deacon Reid's. After calling her friend, Cleotis and not receiving an answer, she dialed another number on the telephone. "Hello, Dennis, I apologize for calling you so late, but Deacon Reid is missing. I'm worried, can you and Louise come over?" she asked. The urgency in her cracked voice was unsettling. Without asking any questions, the young couple changed out of their night attire and rushed to her house.

Mrs. Caldwell did not want to leave the house for fear of missing a telephone call, so when Dennis and Louise appeared, she asked them to search the block for any signs of Deacon Reid. She described his 1949 dark blue Chevy with a dent toward the front end on the passenger's side. "I can't remember his license plate number, but I believe it starts with F53," she acknowledged.

Her incessant pacing was driving her crazy. She took the telephone directory out and looked up the telephone numbers of the two local liquor stores. The first store did not answer, therefore, she assumed it was closed for the evening. A clerk at the second store answered the telephone, announcing that they were closing. Mrs. Caldwell explained that Deacon Reid was missing. "He's sixty-eight years old, with a brown hat and brown tweed suit, cheerful looking eyes, full round face with a gray mustache and thick glasses. He is medium tall, muscular, and walks side to side with an old man gait." Fastidiously, she rattled out her description of him without hesitation. The clerk responded that she had not seen him, but asked the other employees if they had served him. One of the clerks recalled waiting on a man fitting her description a few hours before.

Mrs. Caldwell called Cleotis, and this time he promptly answered the phone.

"Flora, I've been trying to reach you, but your phone has been busy."

"I'm sorry. Did you find him?"

"No one has seen him. I checked the parking lot for his car, but I didn't have any luck. The building is on alert and we have gone door-to-door to ask if anyone has spotted him. The security guard here promised to call me if he shows up."

"Oh my God, where is he?" she asked panic stricken.

Stabbing pains raced through her chest, causing her to gasp for air as she held her bosom and fell back in her chair. She inhaled, and then exhaled deeply ending with a sigh. "So far I've been able to find out he went to Forrest Liquors," she continued, but her response was brimmed with fear. "I guess it's time to call the police, he must have been in a car accident."

"I'm coming over," said Cleotis.

"No! You need to stay there just in case Rufus shows up."

"No, I don't. I can have the guard call us at your house, if he does."

Once Dennis and Louise returned from searching up and down the block, Mrs. Caldwell informed them that Deacon Reid had been sighted at the liquor store. After expressing her fear regarding him being involved in a car accident, they agreed her assumption was plausible. Dennis volunteered to go out and search for him, while Louise stayed to console Mrs. Caldwell.

Ignoring the nagging pain in her chest, Mrs. Caldwell called the police and waited in the living room with Louise. When they heard someone running up the stairs, with high expectations, Mrs. Caldwell ran to the door with Louise trailing close behind her. To their disappointment, it was Cleotis coming to join them.

)0(

Dennis parked his truck behind a squad car in front of Mrs. Caldwell's house after searching for Deacon Reid. He ran up the stairs, found Mrs. Caldwell's door ajar, and bolted in the house interrupting a questioning police officer. All eyes turned toward him.

One of the two police officers asked, "Who are you?"

Mrs. Caldwell intervened by saying, "He is my tenant. Dennis, did you have any luck?"

Dennis reported, "Deacon Reid's car is sitting on the corner three doors away from the liquor store, but there aren't any signs of him. His car is locked and seemed undisturbed."

"Where is this liquor store?" asked the oldest and stockiest officer.

After Dennis informed them of its location, the officer said, "We'll go take a look, but I want all of you to stay here until we get back, just in case we have additional questions."

)0(

Both officers drove off in their squad car to the location of Deacon Reid's car to inspect it. The street was quiet and all the stores were closed. A few businesses were dimly lit and there was no activity on the street, not even a passing vehicle. Inspecting Deacon Reid's Chevy, they flashed their flashlights into it and returned to Iroquois Street.

The police officers did not want to make a report because there was not enough evidence that anything was wrong.

"Mr. Reid could have met up with a friend and rode with him or her somewhere," said the oldest officer.

"Didn't you say you had an argument with him?" commented the taller officer who had been quiet throughout their visit.

"Yes, but…," replied Mrs. Caldwell.

"Well, he probably met up with someone and needed to blow off some steam," interrupted the same officer.

The police officers looked at each other with an all-knowing smirk. The group understood exactly what the officer was implying and they were appalled by their implications. Mrs. Caldwell threw a tantrum. She shouted, "Isn't it obvious, you nincompoops, that the poor man is somewhere hurt! Something bad has happen to him! I'd appreciate it, if you would get off your lazy duffs and go and find him!" Her quiet mannered voice disappeared, replaced by a high pitch strident that sounded so unnatural even to her that it trembled as she spoke. Her stubbornness did not allow the tears that wanted to escape from her eyes. Only after her outburst, did the police officers agree to investigate further.

20

By 1:00 a.m., the phone rang and Mrs. Caldwell rushed to answer it. The caller was a nurse from the emergency room of Central University Hospital. She announced that Rufus Reid advised her to call.

"What happened to him?" Mrs. Caldwell wanted to know.

The nurse explained, "A family was driving by when they saw Mr. Reid stagger and fall onto the street. Initially, they thought he was drunk until he shouted for help. They helped him into their automobile and brought him to the hospital. He passed out in their vehicle and remained in that condition until a while ago. He has been asking for you."

"Can I talk to him?" asked Mrs. Caldwell.

"I'm sorry, but there isn't a phone close to him."

"Tell him I'm on my way there. Thank you."

She rode with Cleotis in his automobile and Dennis and Louise followed them in their truck.

Mrs. Caldwell was the only person allowed to see him, and she was horrified when she saw him lying on a stretcher. Devastated, but relieved, Mrs. Caldwell felt as if she had aged ten years, and the pain in her chest finally began to dissipate. She stood in the background and observed Deacon Reid while a physician examined him. The physician explained as he continued with his examination, "His head is swollen due to contusions, his jaw and several ribs seemed to be fractured, and his right hand appears broken. I'm sending him up for x-rays." After the doctor finished, he instructed Mrs. Caldwell not to allow Deacon Reid to talk too much.

Mrs. Caldwell stood by the bed and touched Deacon Reid on his arm. Leaning toward him she kissed him lightly on his forehead before she asked, "Oh Rufus, what happened?" Their eyes locked and a bond that was always there, but never expressed by either one of them, touched the core of their souls. Their unspoken words revealed the passion they shared and the air was thick from it.

As two streams joining at a bend, Mrs. Caldwell spoke first, "I love you and was so worried about you. I knew something terrible had happened to you. I would have never been able to forgive myself if I didn't have the chance to tell you how I feel about you."

It hurt for him to speak. His watery eyes overflowed and tears rolled down his chubby cheeks. "I've known all along that we loved each other. I've been waiting for you to come around," he replied.

Although his words were barely audible, it was not difficult for her to understand him. Her resistant wall of stubbornness and independence melted, opening a passageway for the proliferation of their love.

"I was jumped by two men after I left the liquor store," he winced in agony.

"What! Did you see them?"

"No, one of them wore a ski mask. I fought back Flora, but there were two of them. They took my wallet and the bottle of whiskey I bought was broken in the scuffle," he explained before being swished away by the orderly for x-rays.

"Rufus I was so afraid. I'm glad you're safe, I'll be waiting here for you when you return," she promised, her voice trailing down the hall after him.

Mrs. Caldwell had lost one man to a tragic accident and once again, she was faced with the pain and anguish of possibly losing another. What was it about her that acted as a magnet, attracting such pain and suffering? Her categorical opinion was if no one else had ever been in this kind of predicament. Her sentiment led her to believe that she was being tested to see if she could endure the pain. "Dear Lord," she prayed, "thank you for bringing Rufus back to me safely." Wearily, she sat in the chair in the room and bellowed hard sobs. Gathering her wits, she returned to the others to report what she discovered. She advised them to go home and she would remain at the hospital. Dennis and Louise left, but promised to check on her and Deacon Reid during the day. Cleotis opted to stay with her.

)0(

At home in their bed, Louise asked, "Dennis, who could have assaulted Deacon Reid? If they wanted to rob him, they didn't have to beat him up too."

"I don't know, Lou. He's a strong man. It sounds as if he put up a good fight."

"Mrs. Caldwell was frightened, I hated seeing her so distraught."

"I'm in agreement with you, but everything is going to be alright. Let's try and get some sleep. We've got to get up in a few hours," said Dennis.

"I'll come home for lunch and check on Mrs. Caldwell."

"She'll probably be at the hospital. After work we can go to the hospital and see how Deacon Reid is doing."

21

"Louise, this neighborhood had always been a quiet one. I've always felt safe here," said Mr. Hirsch while straightening up the things on the counter, after hearing about Deacon Reid from Louise. "I've been at this location over thirty years and never heard of anything like this happening. Of course, we get spousal disputes, an occasion drunk, but beating up a man and robbing him? Now that's just unheard of!" He conveniently chose not to inform her that he moved from the area when the neighborhood ethnically changed. "I sure hope this isn't the beginning of a change for the worse."

"So do I. My Dennis and I have been happy living here," commented Louise.

By early afternoon, the news of Deacon Reid's assault spread throughout the community. The police knew the exact location where the attack took place. No witnesses came forward and all the community could do was to be vigilant.

Mrs. Rice, a thin elderly woman wearing a funning looking hat entered the fabric store, asking, "Did you hear what happened in front of Gallagher's Real Estate Company last night? A poor elderly man was beaten up and robbed."

"Yes," replied another customer, who had been quietly scanning through bolts of materials in one of the aisles.

"It seems to me that someone at the liquor store should have heard something," insisted Mrs. Haynes, a young mother with her baby next to her in a stroller.

"I won't be coming out after dark," replied Mrs. Rice.

"Well, I'm not going to let this stop me from doing what I have to do," said a short figured woman with an abundance of hips in a smock top. She displayed her defiance by waving her finger in the air.

"We'll just have to be careful and maybe travel in groups," suggested Mrs. Haynes.

Louise felt sorry that Deacon Reid had to be the topic of their conversation. Proudly, she defended his honor by informing them how bravely he fought back.

The gossip reminded her of her hometown where news spread swiftly. She had not expected this in a large city like Los Angeles, but somehow this section of the city had isolated itself. Louise realized that the people were as closely knit as those in Avinger. *It feels comfortable being here*, she contemplated, *At least up until now*. Baffled by the robbery, she couldn't come up with anything substantial enough to explain it, nor could she push it to the back of her mind. *Why would anyone want to rob Deacon Reid? Why not rob someone with money, a fancy car, and expensive clothes?*

Before leaving for lunch, Louise dialed the hospital to check on Deacon Reid. Her call was transferred to the intensive care unit, where a nurse informed her that he was recovering, but was in severe pain. Rushing home for lunch, she stopped at Mrs. Caldwell's and found her at home resting. Mrs. Caldwell informed her, "Rufus is stable, and his prognosis is good. His chest is bound tight due to multiple fractures, and his hand is in a cast. This morning he is scheduled to have his jaw set with wire and it will be much more difficult for him to speak. He'll remain in the hospital for weeks," she added. Plagued by the assault as much as Louise was, she asked, "Did they think that an elderly man on the street at night would be carrying a lot of money? The poor man doesn't have much, but of course, the thieves wouldn't have known that," she rattled on.

Mrs. Caldwell surmised that the attackers came from outside of their community. She prepared lunch for Louise while they discussed the incident further. "It just doesn't make sense," Mrs. Caldwell continued.

Louise expressed the same sentiments, and in their frustration, they were thankful that matters were not worse. Louise returned to work and Mrs. Caldwell left shortly thereafter to spend the afternoon with Deacon Reid.

)0(

First thing in the morning, Paul made a visit to the hardware store and got the tools he thought would assist him in jimmying the locks and opening the doors. Subsequent to Mrs. Caldwell's departure, he and Mark went down the backstairs and began to work on opening her backdoor. With Mark as the lookout, Paul conscientiously, set about to the business of picking the lock. Mark watched over his shoulder as he positioned his tools down beside him in a particular manner. "What you *gonna* do, sit down and have a plate of food or *somethin'? Haennnnn!*" asked Mark chuckling at Paul's preparation. Arrogantly, Paul frowned at him. Careful not to cause noticeable damage to the door, after a half hour with no success, Paul demonstrated his exacerbation by banging his hand on the door.

"Damn fucking door!" he cursed.

"Let me try it. *Haennnnn!*" suggested Mark. His cocky sneer annoyed Paul.

"Okay hot shot! Let's see if you can do any better."

Mark did not have the patience that was required, and he left dents and scratches on the lock and door. After another half hour, Mark was ready to give up.

"Let's just bust the door open with the crowbar!" he finally said.

"We can't! We can't afford to take the chance. Suppose the bullion isn't in her apartment. We don't need to draw unnecessary attention to ourselves. We'll have to wait," said Paul.

After several more vexing attempts on the door, Paul suggested going to inspect Dennis and Louise's backyard since they had been interrupted before. Poking a thin iron rod into the soil and finding nothing, they concentrated their efforts on the newly built shed. Not only were they concerned about what was in the shed, but what was possibly beneath it. Paul found a shovel in Mrs. Caldwell's backyard and the men took turns digging deep holes under and around Dennis' shed. Their clumsiness knocked it over on its side making everything fall inside it. Dennis had installed a padlock, so they were unable to rearrange the mess they made. To conceal their digging, they patted the soil down the best they could before repositioning the shed. Paul knocked the dirt off the shovel and returned it to its original spot.

They tried breaking into Dennis and Louise's house but encountered the same problem that they had with Mrs. Caldwell's lock. They argued amongst themselves blaming each other for not knowing what to do.

"Hell, you spent more time in jail than I did. You should have learned by now how to crack a goddamn door lock!" shouted Mark in annoyance.

"Fuck you!" was the reply he received from Paul, who was hot and sweaty.

He did not like hard work and he was tired. Cleaning the railroad cars was bad enough without this added irritation. At least when they cleaned the cars they used water and chemicals. This was plain old black dirt filled with worms, ants, and numerous crawling creatures that gave him the creeps. He should have worn gloves. His fingernails were dirty, he was musty, and his shoes and clothes were filthy. For the moment, he could not stand the sight of Mark, and they were running out of time because someone would be returning home soon.

"How can we explain this mess without admitting that we did not see or at least hear the culprits? *Haennnnn!*" asked Mark.

"Shut up, asshole!" "Take off you shoes, climb the stairs, and take a shower! We've got to get out of here before they come home! Hurry up!"

Like a puppy dog, Mark obeyed him because he feared Paul's wrath. Paul made one last attempt to trigger the lock before following Mark's footsteps, but this time his hold on the pick fumbled causing him to stab himself in the hand. Profanely, he cursed as his disposition worsened.

Quickly, they cleaned up their mess and packed for travel. Gathering their dirty clothes and shoes, Paul drove to a laundromat nearby to wash them. They set up house for the night with a couple of whores who were acquaintances of Mark's and who could be used as alibis, if necessary.

22

Upon arriving home from work, Louise stopped by Mrs. Caldwell's house. After knocking on her door and getting no response, Louise left assuming she was at the hospital. She went home and made a quick meal of sandwiches and a salad for her and Dennis to eat before going to the hospital to visit Deacon Reid. When Dennis arrived, he kissed Louise intimately on her lips, clutching her tightly.

"Oh no you don't, mister!" she responded playfully, using her arms to keep him from touching her. "Have you forgotten we've someplace to go? Besides, you're filthy. Let go of me! I ran you some bath water, now scoot," she giggled using her hands to shoo him away.

"You're such a spoilsport," he chuckled, reluctantly moving away from her.

He left the bathroom door open and shouted out to her, "How was your day?"

Louise joined him by leaning against the doorframe and watching him bathe. "It was busy, which was fine with me. I checked in a large shipment of merchandise that I catalogued and priced for a big sale we're having. Mr. Hirsch is going to allow me to advertise it by putting up sale signs in the windows. I'm making them in the back of the store and so far they look pretty good."

"When are you having the sale?"

"Next Saturday so the signs have to be finished by tomorrow. I learned how to use his mimeograph machine to make flyers and I will pass them out to our customers. I want to see if some of the stores will allow me to put them in their windows or on their counters."

"That's an excellent idea! I think I'll stop by the store on the day of the sale to see how you're doing," he said, earnestly, proud of his wife as he listened to her new terminology.

He finished his bath and Louise helped him dry his back. "Nice backside you have here," she commented as she pressed her breast against him. He turned to face her, "Nice front too if I may say so," she added focusing on his masculinity. Playfully, she jumped backward to maintain a safe distance, when he tried to snatch her. She retreated to the kitchen, communicating over her shoulder she said, "Enough of that or we'll never get out of the house. Dinner is ready, come and eat as soon as you get dressed."

)0(

Louise drove to the hospital, allowing Dennis some time to unwind. "Hon, I'm nervous about this whole thing. Mr. Hirsch and the customers at the store couldn't stop talking about what happened to Deacon Reid. Everyone was surprised that something like this could happen in our neighborhood," she said referring to the abstruse attack.

"Me and some of the guys at work were talking about it, and they said that you can expect things like this to happen occasionally. You have to watch your back, but more so in other sections of the city."

"People are shocked, just the same."

"I don't think we have anything to worry about, Lou."

In the back of Louise's mind the situation lingered, she was not convinced. During the remainder of the trip, they rode in silence consumed with their private thoughts.

Hospital policy only allowed two visitors at a time to see a patient. Louise went first and found Mrs. Caldwell in the room sitting by the window reading her Bible while Deacon Reid slept peacefully. Her landlord looked up into her eyes and extended her arms. Louise bent over to embrace her before occupying the empty chair next to her. The older woman distraughtly sobbed and muttered words of relief. Louise urged her to leave the room so that they could speak freely without disturbing Deacon Reid. In the corridor, Louise held Mrs. Caldwell, comforting and reassuring her that things would workout. Positioned by a medicine cart in the hall, a nurse stood observing the women. She asked if everything was alright. With her arm across Mrs. Caldwell's shoulders, Louise looked up and responded that they were okay, then thanked the nurse for her concern.

Mrs. Caldwell advised Louise, "Deacon Reid has been sleeping off and on and is in pain. The doctor said he'll be fine. A police officer came to visit him and although Rufus had trouble talking, he told us everything he could remember regarding the attack. The officer said the assailants must have observed him entering the store and lain in wait for him. He happened to arrive at a time when they were waiting to prey upon an unsuspecting customer and they undoubtedly chose him. The officer commended him for his bravery and wished him a speedy recovery. All that matters is that he's *gonna* to be alright and I'm *gonna* take care of him when he gets out of here. I can't bear the thought of living without him."

Mrs. Caldwell greeted Dennis in the reception area and then left for the evening. Louise and Dennis stayed a while and talked to Deacon Reid as if he was awake. Deacon Reid opened his eyes and smiled acknowledging their presence, but succinctly returned to a twilight nap.

The couple sat in silence until Louise let out a sigh, saying, "Deacon Reid, do hurry up and heal. Mrs. Caldwell loves you and she needs to show you how much."

"I know," he murmured, grimacing in pain when he tried to smile.

Dennis gently patted his shoulder before they departed, promising to return in a few days. That night in Dennis' arms, Louise fell into a restless slumber, troubled by the incident and at how closely they were involved in it.

23

After dropping Louise off to work, Dennis went to the lumberyard and hardware store, where he priced the materials he needed to do the work on Mrs. Caldwell's attic. Upon entering his backyard, he noticed that his tool shed was standing slightly off center and wondered why it was not noticeable before now. Inspecting it, he discovered that the shed had been tampered with even though the lock remained unbroken. Curiosity, not rage led him to unlock the door hastily. Jerking it open, caused it to swing back and forth hitting him in the face. Dumbfounded, he watched some of his tools tumble out onto the ground and was thankful that he had assiduously anchored the shelves to the walls.

Who could have done this? Due to the weight of the shed with its contents, one man alone could not have done the damage. It would have taken at least two men or several strong children to move it. In a faded plaid shirt and his favorite pair of overalls, he stood scratching his head trying to figure out when was the last time he used the shed. *Sunday afternoon it was fine.* A week had passed, since all the excitement, and that was his logical explanation for not noticing the shed's present condition.

Leaning against the shed with his hand, he noticed that it sat unsteady and the soil underneath it had been disturbed. As a matter-of-fact, the soil in the immediate area had been tampered with and flattened. Somebody had covertly attempted to conceal their digging. Fixated by paranoia, he searched for other clues of disturbance. Examining each window and the entrance of his coach house, Dennis noticed scratch marks on the doors and locks. From what he could ascertain, the rest of the yard had not been bothered.

Walking around Mrs. Caldwell's house, Dennis industriously assessed her windows and front doors. He mounted the stairs to her back porch to examine her door and found scratch marks on the door and lock. Contemporaneously, the marks could have appeared or they could have already been there. Dennis did not dare ask Mrs. Caldwell about them for fear of upsetting her. He walked up to the second floor and knocked on Paul & Mark's door to ask them if they had heard or seen anything. Not receiving an answer, he automatically inspected their door and there were no visible mars or scratches.

Analytically, he resolved the disturbance could have occurred anytime during the week. The tools in the shed were valuable to him, he could not imagine them being that important to anyone else, therefore, he surmised it was the handiwork of kids at play. Although Dennis was not completely ready to admit openly that someone was in search of the treasure, he was unable to cast aside his reservations otherwise. He hated having to mention his discovery to Louise, because he did not want to alarm her with anymore worrisome developments. Consequently, he determined it was necessary to inform her so that she could be on guard for any trouble that might surface. His wife would insist that she could defend herself, but he knew better. After all, look what happened to Deacon Reid.

)0(

When Louise arrived home, she announced, "What a pleasant surprise," after finding supper waiting for her. "I forgot you knew how to cook," she said cheerfully to Dennis.

"I can probably cook better than you, but I don't want to upset the harmonious balance between our chores," he mocked.

"You're probably right, with parents like yours who've taught you everything," she chortled.

)0(

"Lou, I have something important to discuss with you," he said after cutting a piece of meat. "This morning I discovered that someone tried to break in our house and upset my tool shed. The shed had been knocked over and dug under. Someone smoothed the dirt out and tried to make it appear as if it had never been touched. Although, they weren't able to open it, the door was pulled from its hinges with a crowbar or something. When I opened it, the tools fell out on the ground.

Louise stopped eating, unaware that she held her fork with food on it in mid-air between her plate and her mouth. Astounded, she listened to her husband relay his story. Somewhere between the words "knocked over the shed and dug underneath it," she stopped listening. Her anger intensified.

She interrupted, "Dennis, they are looking for the treasure." It was unequivocally clear to her who was responsible. "I bet you didn't find scratch marks on Mark and Paul's door."

That bothered him as well, but he rationalized by saying, "Someone probably interrupted whomever was here."

"Because they didn't call the police or say anything to Mrs. Caldwell or to us?" said Louise completing Dennis' statement. "Now, come on Dennis, you aren't that gullible. Why can't you admit that the culprits are Mark and Paul? It makes plenty of sense to me. Since they live here maybe no one thought it was odd for them to be digging in the yard, but someone should have, for that very reason."

Refusing to accept Louise's accusation, Dennis remarked, "Now Lou, don't start jumping off the handle and accusing them again.

"Dennis, I know what I'm talking about!"

"No you don't! I haven't seen them in over a week!."

"Precisely! They don't want us to know what they've been up to!"

"Stop it, Lou!"

"No, Dennis, I won't! Those men normally travel on the road for ten to fourteen days at a time and then they are home for at least four to five days before heading out again. They arrived on Friday and were home on Sunday night." Louise spoke rapidly.

"How do you know that?"

"I make it a point of keeping track of them because I don't trust Ma…, them," she corrected herself, careful not to give Dennis any cause to approach Mark for his inappropriate behavior.

"Lou, you're making a mountain out of a mole hill!"

"No, I'm not! I don't like the way they look at me!"

"You're an attractive woman, who wouldn't want to look at you," replied Dennis.

"A neighbor who lives on the same property should respect a man's wife. They don't, especially Mark!" she blurted out, realizing she had said too much.

Suddenly, cognitive of what Louise was saying, Dennis stopped arguing with her. His eyes narrowed, grew darker, and his gaze seemed to pierce into her soul. "Okay, what happened, and I'm only asking once," he demanded. Louise knew Dennis' temper could flare up to the point of him causing bodily harm to someone. Although she never experienced it first hand, she had heard how someone crossed him, and he had broken a man's arm over his knee. Her only hope was to explain what transpired between her and Mark in a nonchalant manner that would not rile him.

Forcing herself to look directly into his threatening face she said, "The night that I went over to Mrs. Caldwell's house to ask her to keep an eye on the house for us, Mark was leaving out." Judiciously choosing her words, she continued, "He teased me and wouldn't let me pass him by blocking my way."

Pushing his unfinished plate of food aside, Dennis moved back from the table and crossed his legs to listen closely. He observed her objectively.

"What did you do?" he spoke austerely.

"I told him to move out of my way, which he did, but he was compelled to tell me how nice looking I was before allowing me up the stairs."

"Did he touch you?" Dennis' skin appeared taut and his expression serious and menacing.

"No, silly. He didn't touch me."

"That was the night you asked me for a knife wasn't it? It was meant for him."

"Well, yeah, just in case he really tried to get fresh with me," explained Louise.

"And that's all that happened?"

"Yes, Dennis, nothing else happened."

With equanimity he said, "I'm sure he was just teasing you, but if you ever feel threatened by him, Lou, don't hesitate to tell me."

"Don't worry, darling, I won't."

Relieved that their discussion was over, Louise decided against any further comments with him regarding the men's involvement with the treasure. It was an uncomfortable position to find herself in. For the time being, she determined it was wiser to be cautious and trust her own instincts, since she didn't have anyone else to confide in.

To Louise's surprise Dennis said, "Lou, you may be right about someone trying to find the treasure, maybe I should put bars around the doors and windows."

"That would only draw more attention to our house. It would be declaring that we have something of value, but what else can we do?" she asked.

"Let's move it in the middle of the night. I can bury it under Mrs. Caldwell's house."

"No, you can't do that, someone might see you." Especially Mark and Paul she wanted to add because she knew they watched the coach house from their apartment windows every chance they got.

"Let's leave it where it is for now, but promise me you'll be careful and will communicate with me if you notice anything unusual."

"I promise," she said. Louise secretly schemed to conduct her own investigation starting in the backyard.

24

After Dennis left for work, Louise did not return to bed as usual. Instead, she threw on a purple blouse and a pair of black slacks and headed for the yard. Before leaving the house, she looked out the kitchen window toward the second floor to make sure she was not being watched. In her own section of the yard, she examined Dennis' shed and the soil around it. Then she strolled toward Mrs. Caldwell's house, mindfully glancing toward the second floor. As she passed Mrs. Caldwell's shed, she noticed a shovel resting against it. Approaching the shed, she studied the shovel and found dirt still on it. The dirt matched the sandy color and density of the soil around Dennis' shed. The farmer in her made her boldly go and pick up handfuls of soil around the flowers and vegetables. Studying the soil, Louise noticed that it was darker and richer due to the fertilizer Mrs. Caldwell used. She surmised that Mrs. Caldwell's shovel was used to dig around Dennis' shed. When she finished, she rubbed her hands together dusted off the soil, and wiped her hands on the sides of her pants.

Louise looked toward Mrs. Caldwell's house and was quite prepared to answer any questions if the older woman saw her. If need be, she would fabricate a story about having difficulty growing one of her vegetables and wanted to compare the soil. Moving stealthily, she mounted the back stairs leading to the porch and snuck up to the second floor. Someone had made a poor attempt to sweep away dirt from the stairs and when she reached the second floor landing, she found more dirt around the door and in the crevices of the door's threshold.

Jiggling the doorknob, Louise discovered that the door was unlocked. She smiled with satisfaction.

Certain that the men were not in the apartment, she knocked on the door just in case, before pushing it open. "Hello? Is anyone home?" she asked boldly, peeping her head inside. As she anticipated, there was silence. Louise removed her shoes and in her bare feet, she entered the kitchen of the apartment quietly.

The kitchen was tidy with only a few dishes in the sink, not at all, what she expected, because men were usually slobs when it came to the kitchen. Louise wiggled her toes as she paced across the floor. The kitchen floor was gritty with dirt from the yard, not from the ordinary dust that would accumulate in a house. With her hand, she dusted off her feet before venturing further into the apartment. Off to the right of the kitchen was a bedroom with the view of the backyard. She assumed it belonged to Mark, since he spent much of his time looking out of its window. Haphazardly, his clothing was thrown in piles on the floor and some of it rested on a chair. The room smelled of stale cigarettes and alcohol. On the dresser were empty beer and soda bottles and an ashtray was overflowing with cigarette butts. The bed was unmade and an empty cigarette wrapper was left lying on top of it. She shook her head. The wincing thought of rummaging through Mark's things did not set well with her, so she decided to forego it and only return to search through them, if she had to.

The bathroom had a faint smell of urine. Grimacing with amazement, she gazed at the unforeseen sight of the spotless sink and the bathtub without a bathtub ring. Matter-of-fact as she scrutinized the room, it was tidy and that was also surprising. Proceeding down the hall and reaching the second bedroom, again she was taken aback. Although it was obviously a man's room, it appeared to have a feminine touch. The draperies were pale green with golden thread intertwined throughout, which matched the damask of the silk bedspread. It was even more fashionable than Mrs. Caldwell's draperies. She was certain that the room was decorated to fit Paul's taste and that the furnishings were things he brought with him when he moved in. Not a thing was out of place. Sniffing the air, Louise received a pleasant whiff of a cigar, which she undoubtedly felt was costly because all the cigars she ever smelled were nauseating. Walking over to inspect his closet, she found stylish suits and silk lounging robes, something like what she had seen worn by male actors who portrayed an affluent man at the picture show or males in a high fashion magazine. On the floor was a couple of pair of highly polished dress shoes.

This was a mystery in itself. There was definitely more to Paul than she realized and apprehension nagged her. *Who is this man and why is he traveling with Mark? Was Mark really his son? He certainly didn't act like him nor did he resemble him. What are they up to? Were they the ordinary run-of-the mill thieves as she suspected them to be, or were they some kind of spies working undercover for the government? Don't be foolish,* she scolded. *Paul is a confidence man, a lady's man, the type of scoundrel that preyed on old ladies and other non-suspecting souls.* The type of which she had no experience with, none other than what she had seen at the movies or read about in books. Somewhere, somehow, he picked up Mark along the way and they became companions.

Ker plunk! She heard from a distance. Louise jerked around, ran to the living room, and cautiously looked out of the window. The men's car was nowhere in sight. It was only a boy on a bicycle riding down the street delivering the morning newspapers after throwing the latest edition on the stairs of Mrs. Caldwell's front porch. With a big sigh of relief, she returned to Paul's bedroom. Careful not to disrupt the things in his bureau she went through each drawer, hoping to find some clues to aid her. She found check stubs from the railroad company made out to a Kevin Tatum and various receipts to the same name. *So this is your real name.* When she reached the last drawer, she ran her hand through Paul's clothing and found papers in the bottom of the drawer. Taking care not to upset anything, she sprawled out on the floor and read through the papers in front of her. There were documents showing Kevin Tatum's release from prison, dated less than a year ago. Among these papers were letters from female admirers with the faintest hint of perfume, addressed to him at two different addresses in Los Angeles and San Francisco.

It is obvious that Paul/Kevin is the brain of their operation. Of course he is. The weasel only thinks with his dick, Louise deliberated with abhorrence. Probing around for more clues, a shelf in the closet caught her eye. On her tiptoes, she reached up and felt the cold steel of what she was sure was a revolver. Clump! Clump! Someone was coming up the stairs and she had to hide. Panicking, Louise realized she had left her shoes on the back porch. With no time to retrieve them, she entered the closet, leaving the door partially ajar. It creaked as it moved. "Damn!" she whispered. *I'm a goner.* Clump! Clump! The footsteps were getting closer. Easing toward the far corner of the closet, Louise crouched down on her knees. *If I'm discovered, they'll kill me for sure.*

Her heart pulsated with fear and the heat and poor air circulation from the closet did not help. Gasping for air, the drum roll pounding of her heart made her chest heave, feeling as if it were about to burst. Her upper torso was drenched in sweat. To control her breathing, Louise forced herself to take slow deep breaths, she mused over the seriousness of her situation. *If they kill me, they'd kill my baby too. Why have I been so foolish?* She remained curled up waiting to be exposed. Horrid visions of being caught and shot by the very gun she just found, or perhaps knifed or bludgeoned to death plagued her in her anguish. Would she ever see Dennis again and their unborn child? Can she get out of this unharmed? Clump! Clump!

25

Deacon Rufus Reid grew up in Georgia in a rural town outside of Macon. One of five children, as he grew into manhood, he tired of farm life. Getting his hands dirty and doing hard work did not bother him. He just loathed farming, therefore, when he got the opportunity to do something different, he did. In the midst of spring, he made an impulsive decision to join a traveling minister, assisting him in establishing outdoor church revivals throughout the country. When they reached Los Angeles, he was so besotted by the city that he made the decision to stay. The climate was similar to Georgia's, but the atmosphere was unique and exciting. Californians exhibited an open-minded way of thinking that was suitable to him. Leaving the minister, he remained in the boarding house the minister arranged for them to live in. Jobs were plentiful and he obtained work in various factories, all of which sustained him. Requiring more financial stability, he sought employment in a trade and he was accepted as a plumbing apprentice. After putting in long hours for several years, he became a certified plumber. Other than taking an occasional job on his own, he was satisfied working at Acme Plumbing until his retirement a few years ago.

When his mother passed away, he traveled back to Georgia to bury her and to help his siblings settle her affairs. Their father died several years before, and since Rufus was the elder sibling that empowered him to make certain that everyone got a fair share of their parent's estate. It should have been a simple matter of divvying up the property and/or selling it and sharing the profits. Some of his siblings thought that since they had spent more time taking care of their aging parents or farming the land after the others moved away that they were entitled to more than the others. His sisters wanted personal items that they swore that their mother had promised them, but there was no proof. Since there was no will to speak of, Rufus took on the confrontational task as the unofficially appointed mediator because probate court was not something colored folks or the "poor Joe" dealt with. That was something for the white folks with money. He sent a message to his boss via Western Union, asking his permission to take a leave of absence from his job until he could settle his mother's estate.

)0(

His sisters took after his dad's side of the family with full buxom chests, proportioned waists, and big heavy bottoms. When he angered them, Rufus envisioned them sitting on him and crushing the life out of him. In childhood, his sisters were rivals and constantly bickered over each other's things. Both sisters had husbands that loved them and amazingly got along well with them. His sisters learned quickly how to keep their husbands content by cooking fantastic meals, pampering them, and keeping their children in line so they would not be bothersome. In their presence Rufus heard several "yes Mable, yes dear, yes Clara whatever you want, I'll do it," from both of the men. Rufus and his brothers could not understand them being henpecked, but both men seemed satisfied. They worked hard, bringing their money home for their wives to manage. What was even more sickening was when he watched his sisters manipulate their husbands, making each think that he came up with a suggestion on his own. Rufus wondered whether this was a secret weapon mothers taught their daughters.

His sisters were conniving and always got their way with their parents. They would take turns instigating fights with the boys, after which they assumed the falsehood of the sweet innocent victims.

This infuriated him and his brothers because their parents always believed his sisters.

Once while performing his fiduciary duties, Rufus yanked a hat that belonged to his mother from his two argumentative sisters, resulting in him tearing the hat and ruining it. He was so appalled by their behavior that he threatened to put them both over his knees and beat the living stew out of them. When they voiced their complaints to their husbands, both men bowed out, implying it was a family matter and that they would have to work out their differences. His brothers fought over fishing equipment and tools, while all of them fought over personal items they each wanted as keepsakes.

It took him a few months to resolve their differences, resulting in settlement agreements that pleased everyone. As arbitrator, poor Rufus sat between them and article-by-article he equally divided the things, using the old selection method of one for you and one for him. This method proved to be helpful in resolving many of the "I want this or Mama promised me that or Daddy said I could have those" matters. It taught him before departing this life, to leave a will to avoid heated disputes. Since the majority of them had relocated to cities and did not want the property, he sold lumber off the land before putting the land up for sale. Dividing the assets amongst them, one of his brothers chose to reside in their parents' house and maintain a few acres. He was a retired schoolteacher and in his retirement, he farmed a small portion of the land and took up raising rabbits. An annual family gathering was held at his house and all of the siblings and their families attended.

At one of these gatherings, Rufus met his future wife. Her genial nature and infectious laughter made him realize what he was missing in his life. She attended the same church as his brother's wife and Rufus continued a long distance relationship with her by corresponding through the mail. After writing each other for almost a year, at the next family gathering with self-assurance, he proposed marriage to her. They married and with his new bride by his side, he returned to Los Angeles. Although Rufus could provide for his new wife comfortably, she was not satisfied with being a housewife. Insistent on employment, she worked as a housekeeper in a hotel in the business district of town for years.

The couple tried to produce children, but never had any luck. Lydia, his wife, had seven miscarriages before finally dying from consumption years ago. Deeply wounded by her death, Rufus never desired to remarry. He found solace in his work and in church, which resulted in his motivation to become a deacon.

As a fairly nice looking man with a profession, he was highly sought after by the churchwomen. His pleasant smile and unmistakable southern voice rang through, displaying his confidence and intelligence. Also courteous and helpful, he was irresistible to the ladies. He did not consider himself neither supercilious nor a professional man, just an average man who worked as a plumber. Comfortable with having an occasional girlfriend, he steered clear of the women from his church and made light of their persistence for his affection. When a relationship became too serious, he withdrew himself emotionally because he did not ever think anyone could replace his wife.

When Deacon Reid met Mrs. Caldwell, her husband was living and both of them were members of his church. After the vehicle accident that took Mr. Caldwell's life, Deacon Reid comforted Flora. During this time, he developed a predilection for her and began to question his own intentions toward her. She awakened exuberant feelings within him that he thought were dormant. Drawn toward her independence, his deference for her cultivated into a bonding he was unprepared for, initially. Coming to grips with his own emotions, he realized that Flora needed a proper time to mourn. Consequently, he waited for the right time to approach her.

After a couple of years, he openly pursued her, but she firmly told him that she admired him as a dear friend and did not think that she could commit to an involvement. He remembered her exact words to him, "Rufus, I love you dearly and will always love you, but not in that way. Can we be lifelong friends?" Her words offended him. Fundamentally, he found himself in the same situation but at the opposite end of the realm because he had cast aside the amorous attention he received from numerous women that had pursued him. With high expectations, he hoped one day that Mrs. Caldwell would come around to his way of thinking. In the meantime, he found gratification being in her presence.

For years, he worked with nothing to spend his money on, except food and rent mainly. He built himself a nice savings account. Rufus had aspirations to travel to Europe or go on a cruise to some exotic land. He heard that in England and France that colored folks were treated better than in the United States, and he wanted to check it out. He chuckled when he thought of taking a French class, particularly at his age. Would people think he was trying to be an uppity Negro? Rufus never expressed these desires to Mrs. Caldwell, because he did not want her to laugh at him. If he ever got her to agree to marriage, he planned on suggesting going to Europe on their honeymoon.

)0(

With plenty of time on his hands, he rested in his hospital bed, replaying the events of his attack. *Why me,* he pondered. The two men were not there when he parked his car on the street. That he was sure of. Why all of a sudden would something like this occur, especially to him? Was he becoming so old and senile that he was incapable of being aware of his surroundings? Was this fate or was it his lack of cautiousness? Why would two men want to jump him? He never carried much money on him. Why didn't they wait until the store was ready to close and get some real money? He had less than five bucks in his pocket after purchasing the liquor for Flora.

Why had he gone to the store in the first place? Surely, the alcohol was not that important. He almost forgot his intended purpose of obtaining Flora's telephone book to get the phone number of her last tenants, including his intention to seduce her. The alcohol was his raison d'être to soften her up, to make her more approachable to the idea. He didn't even get a chance to reach first base. If Flora had not been out of liquor, he would not have been at the store. What made him go to that store instead of the other one? Would it have made a difference? Was it his fate to become a victim of an assault? He was laid up, and would be so for weeks, barely able to talk to Flora and tell her how he felt about her. An urgency to profess his love for her plagued him.

Flora promised to take care of him when he got out of the hospital. He took that to mean that he would be staying at her place until he healed. Perhaps, she would allow him to move in with her permanently. Hospital confinement was torturous, but every part of his body ached. Embarrassed by his weakened condition, he had to admit that he looked forward to her daily visits.

Rufus was also disappointed that he would not be able to help Dennis in constructing the rooms in her attic. Everything was all messed up and his life was in shambles. He had not been in this state in years. Silently, he prayed to God to give him strength to heal and endure the pain. He thanked God for sparing his life because matters could have been worse. Shuttering to think of the worse, he prayed more words of gratitude.

26

Time ticked slowly for Louise, as she remained hunched on her knees in the far corner of the dark closet. The confined space caused perspiration to trickle down her face. Her body felt moist and uncomfortable. After several minutes of augmented silence, the door to the apartment did not open. On her hands and knees, Louise crawled beneath the hanging clothes, venturing out, to see if it was safe. Cautiously, she placed her hand on the closet door, to ease it open. It squeaked, she froze in her tracks. Only when it felt safe, did she strike out again. Tiptoeing into the hall, she could hear the swishing sound of a broom on the top landing outside the front door. *"Amazing grace, how sweet the sound that saved a wretch like me,"* sang Mrs. Caldwell as she worked. Quietly, Louise chuckled at her own foolishness after realizing the sound she heard was Mrs. Caldwell's sweeping. The reprieve made her whole body limp with relief. Regaining her self-confidence, she was convinced that the men were on the road traveling. As she exited the backdoor of the apartment, she took care not to lock the door.

)0(

The day was never-ending for Louise because there was not enough traffic in the store to keep her mind occupied. Her restlessness showed.

"Louise, is everything alright?" asked Mr. Hirsch as he brought two bolts of fabric from the backroom.

"Yes, sir. I'm working on a project at home and I'm antsy to return to it," she replied, not having to lie.

"Anything in particular?" he inquired.

"I'm planting some flowers and I want to arrange them in a unique design in the yard."

"I can't help you there. I don't have any experience in gardening. Since its slow why don't you leave a couple of hours early to get a head start on your project?"

Grinning with delight, she responded, "Are you sure you can do without me?"

"Of course," said Mr. Hirsch with a reassuring smile.

)0(

Louise stopped at Mrs. Caldwell's to check on her. When she was about to knock on the door, the neighbor next door walked out on her porch.

"Hello, Louise," said the woman.

"Hi, Mrs. Blunt."

"If you're looking for Mrs. Caldwell, she left for the hospital some time ago."

"Thanks, I'll catch up with her later," Louise beamed, pleased that she was not there.

"I regretted hearing about Mr. Reid. How could anyone do such a terrible thing, especially to an old man who can't defend himself? What's this world coming to?" asked Mrs. Blunt.

Once again, on Deacon Reid's behalf, Louise proudly defended his honor by enlightening the neighbor on how bravely he resisted.

"You know…," started the woman, "oh, never mind, that's alright."

"What? What were you going to say?"

"Well, those men, those Caucasian tenants of Mrs. Caldwell…I don't…," she faltered. "I'm wondering why they are living here."

"What do you mean?" asked Louise overly enthused with curiosity.

"It's none of my business," Mrs. Blunt continued. She arched her back and placed the back of her hands on her hips, moving her head from side to side, as she spoke. "Mrs. Caldwell has the right to rent her apartment to whomever she wants, but…"

"But what, Mrs. Blunt? Has something happened that caused you to be alarmed?"

"Well…the other day I noticed one of the men walking around the house inspecting it. At first, I thought Mrs. Caldwell asked him to do some work around the house, but I knew better than that, because your Dennis has been working for her. The way the man was checking out the doors and windows made me suspicious."

"Which man, the younger one or the older one?" asked Louise.

"The older one."

"Did he do anything he shouldn't have?"

"No, not really, I just felt he was up to something, especially the way he looked around to see if anyone was watching him. When he saw me, he waved and tried to be cordial, but I just stared at him."

"Did you mention this to Mrs. Caldwell?"

"No, because he wasn't doing anything. I'm just leery of those men. You might consider me a nosey neighbor, but with them being white and all…"

"To be honest with you, Mrs. Blunt, I don't trust either of them. If you see them doing something suspicious, maybe you should tell Mrs. Caldwell or call the police."

"Call the police? He wasn't doing anything wrong, honey, the man was just looking around!"

"Well, in case you do see something that isn't right, please let me know."

"Sure will," concluded the neighbor, turning away to re-enter her house.

)0(

After changing into her purple blouse and dark colored pants, Louise chuckled to herself. This set of clothing had become her "Madame Spy" costume. Louise reappeared in the backyard in a matter of minutes to undertake her forbidden task. Boldly, she walked across the yard straight to the backstairs of Mrs. Caldwell's house without bothering to check if the coast was clear. Overly confident, she kept her shoes on, when she entered the men's apartment.

She walked directly to the closet in Paul's bedroom, the place that consumed her thoughts throughout the day. The door was closed. Louise did not remember closing it, but she knew it had to remain the way she originally found it. Standing with her arms folded and her thumb holding up her chin, now, she was unsure. Tossing her concern aside and waving her hand in the air, she eyed the top shelf of the closet. Louise's determination fortified her that nothing was going to stop her from pursuing her mission. In need of something to stand on, she looked around the room and in the corner she spotted the stuffed Tudor backed chair. It did not appear very heavy, but upon attempting to lift it, she had to exert some force. Deliberating that it was too heavy to carry, Louise decided against dragging it, because it would leave a trail on the carpet. Instead, she retrieved a chair from the kitchen, placed it in front of the closet, and climbed upon it to examine the shelf.

In her haste, as she reached for the gun, it slipped from her fingers. Fearful of it going off, Louise stood on the chair with her hands holding the sides of her head. If the gun went off a bullet could hit her anywhere. In slow motion, she watched the gun tumble down to the floor. *Thumpety, thump!* It landed on the wooden floor of the closet without incidence. With relief, Louise jumped from the chair and bent over to examine it. It was a .38 caliber Colt revolver. She noted its similarity to the shotgun she used at home for hunting. The chambers were empty and that was probably the only reason it did not go off. It was also her good fortune that Mrs. Caldwell was not home because if she was she would have heard the gun hit the floor. Liberated from a near disaster, Louise surmised, *City life is much too dangerous, I'm ready to return home to my former life of serenity.*

Grasping the gun and the large envelope underneath it, she took them to the bed. Before opening and reading the contents of the envelope, she stroked her fingertips across the luxurious bedspread, admiring its beauty. The envelope contained a well-drafted sketch of a map of a ranch with several acres of land in Pasadena with penciled X marks on it. The property belonged to Robert Fitzgerald, a well known cattle rancher according to a copy of a newspaper clipping announcing his death in 1946. There were notes regarding people making statements about Fitzgerald dying, leaving gold and silver bullion that was never discovered. It referred to his address being the same as Mrs. Caldwell's. Disconcertedly, Louise dropped the notes on the bed. Urgently requiring something to write with, she took a pen and a blank piece of crumbled paper from a drawer in the bureau to record the man's name and the address in Pasadena.

As an afterthought, before exiting the apartment, she checked around to make certain that she left it in the same condition that she found it. She decided that the closet door was originally open when she first entered the bedroom because that was the only way she could have seen the shelf inside it. Louise smoothed out the bedspread where she sat and headed for the door.

With the victorious excitement of an uncaged leopard on the loose, she exited the apartment with evidence in her hands, linking the men directly to the treasure. What was she going to do with it? Instantly, she deliberated against telling Dennis about her findings, because he would be furious with her for snooping in the men's apartment and placing herself in harm's way. She began to formulate a plan.

)0(

"Lou, Lou, what in tarnation is on your mind! I've been asking you when you want to go with me to see Deacon Reid," said Dennis in a raised, but not agitated voice.

"I'm sorry," she replied. While washing dishes from their supper, she spied on the second floor of Mrs. Caldwell's house through her kitchen window.

"Is something wrong, babe?" he asked. He stood directly behind her, tilting his head so she could see him as he placed his arms around her waist.

"Uh…I was just wondering if we made a mistake by moving here," she replied, knowing this would deter him from pursuing any further questions.

"I know you have been troubled by the things that have been happening lately, but Lou, everything will be alright. I can assure you." Disliking her thoughts, he asked, "How about going for a walk after you finish the dishes?" quickly changing the subject and stealing a kiss from the side of her neck.

"And how about you grabbing a dish towel and helping me dry the dishes to quicken up this process." She threw the dish towel at him.

27

Concluding his examination on Deacon Reid, the young doctor clad in a gray lab jacket said, "Mr. Reid, you're progressing rather nicely."

"Thanks," uttered Deacon Reid through his wired mouth.

"The medicine he's on makes him drowsy, therefore, he's going to sleep a lot," said the physician, directing his attention to Mrs. Caldwell.

"Will he be on it for a long time?"

"That will depend on Mr. Reid. Without it, he would probably be in too much pain."

"The man knows what he's talking about, Flora," nodded Deacon Reid as he sputtered and turned his head toward her.

"As long as you're comfortable, Rufus, I'm content," Flora said, looking downward as she rearranged the folds in her skirt.

It was Monday afternoon and Mrs. Caldwell sacrificed her visit with him on Sunday to allow church members and some of his other acquaintances time to see him.

"Flora, I missed you yesterday."

"I heard that you had plenty of visitors to keep you company," she commented good-humoredly.

"I did, but it hurt to talk. They did most of the talking. I was glad to see them," he continued, tormented by the difficulty to speak.

Mrs. Caldwell filled him in on the events he missed at church before discussing the things she was doing at home. She relayed her future plans for excursions to the beach and zoo that she wanted them to take her grandchildren on. Deacon Reid was glad she included him in her plans. He asked what she was growing in her garden just to hear her speak. Gardening was one of her favorite topics. In discussing it, she spoke as if her flowers were her children.

"Did you plant any corn this year?" he inquired.

"No, because last year I couldn't keep the squirrels away from it. They love it, you know. One morning I came out and caught a squirrel with an ear of corn wedged between the fence. I watched as he expertly shucked it on each side like he had been doing it for years. All he needed was some butter and salt to make it tastier," she laughed.

Deacon Reid chuckled at her tale. "Flora, that's funny. Oh, it hurts to laugh," he replied splinting his face with the hand that wasn't fractured.

Considering his pain, she pulled her Bible out of her purse and resorted to reading scriptures to him.

"Please be careful," he advised her when she finally left.

)0(

After the nurse took his vital signs and administered his medication, Deacon Reid stared at the ceiling absentmindedly, reflecting upon the afternoon visit. He wanted to ask Flora about her "other two tenants," but did not dare antagonize her. His thoughts concerning the men preoccupied him. Dogmatically, he proclaimed them jailbirds, but how was he going to prove it to her? What bothered him the most was that his confinement in the hospital prohibited him from protecting her. He envisioned himself as her knight in shining amour. What he desired most of all was to be her lover and husband, those were the only things absent in their relationship. They were not getting any younger and this incident was an indication for his necessity to pursue her more aggressively.

His rambling thoughts regarding the assault led him to believe that if there had been only one attacker, he would have handled himself better. Something about his attackers seemed familiar. Was it the way they moved when they walked or was the familiar stench of alcohol from one of their breaths? Neither assailants spoke, while they performed their dirty work on him. As a team, each man knew what was required of the other without speaking a word. The idleness of his confinement made him finally construe that the "other two tenants" and the attackers were one of the same. Could he be certain? Was it their clothing? After all, it was too dark for him to see much. *This is nonsense,* he tried to conclude. The robbery was at the store, not at Flora's house, but then he did not consider the attack a robbery, because they only obtained a sparse wallet with five bucks in it. The men walked away from him leaving him doubled over in pain. It was an afterthought of one of them to return and take his wallet. That bothered him and was the premise for his belief.

His agitation escalated, causing him to shudder with anger, making him hyperventilate. *Flora is in danger!* he declared, thwarted by his fear. With all his strength, he pulled himself up into a sitting position and swung his feet over the side of the bed onto the floor. Glowering in pain, he held his side. *I must call Flora!* Deacon Reid reached for the telephone to warn her. With the receiver in his hand, he stopped himself from dialing her number. *She won't believe me*, he resigned. With his head hung low and his feet spread out beneath him firmly planted on the floor, he resigned in defeat. He tried to take control of his emotions. Consequently, he conjectured that the "other two tenants" were after his Flora. Further, he contrived that the men preyed on older ladies, assuming that their mattresses were full of money, just for their taking. What he could not understand was why they had chosen Flora as their victim. Why choose a black woman instead of an opulent white one, anyone but his precious Flora. If they wanted him out of the way, they'd done a good job because his confinement in the hospital, left him vulnerable.

It was imperative that he warn someone. That person had to be Flora, but how could he convince her or anyone else for that matter of his convictions? Without proof who would be willing to believe the ranting of an old man. In his uncertainty, Deacon Reid rationalized that he would be accused of fabricating a story based upon his loss of pride or embarrassment from losing a battle. No longer of much use to society, he lived in a senior citizen housing complex with other cast-asides because of their aging bodies. Refusing to wallow in sorrow he thought, *Hell, the only reason I quit working was because I was tired and was pressured by my friends to retire, since many of them were.* As capable as any man in the company, he could handle himself well in any situation. Skillful in his craft, he taught endless apprentices and watched them develop proficiently enough to work on their own. Some of them even started their own businesses. *Alright man, be honest with yourself. You retired because the work was too demanding and too heavy.* He did not have the stamina to handle the heavy pipes that he once handled without difficulty. Humiliation made him admit his inadequacies and Deacon Reid was forced to accept that he was no longer the man he used to be. The wells of his eyes overflowed and tears rolled down his cheeks. Old and useless, and now he was relentlessly helpless. Self-pity did not permit him to see the good he had done or the importance of his life. Lightheaded from his medication and troubled thoughts, he stretched out on his back and fell into a languid slumber.

)0(

"Hello, Deacon Reid," announced Dennis and Louise in unison, entering his room, before they settled into the chairs by his bed. Deacon Reid was finishing up his supper and an employee from the kitchen entered the room behind the couple and whisked away his tray.

"How are you feeling?" asked Louise, gently touching his hand.

"I guess I'm feeling better everyday. I'm getting bored in here," he said, even though he knew there was not much he could do in his present state.

"That's not what I heard, mister! The nurses told me that you've been trying to kiss them and lock them up in this room with you!" teased Dennis.

Deacon Reid's eyes lit up, before he replied, "I wish," and they all laughed.

They spent time making small talk and catching him up with their jobs and projects.

)0(

"Talk of your attack has settled down some," said Louise.

Deacon Reid's face grew rigid.

Louise noticed the throbbing of his temples and imagined him gritting his teeth. She asked, "What's the matter? Aren't you glad not to be the center of attention?"

He nodded but muttered, "I believe I know why it has been quiet."

"What do you mean?" interjected Louise.

Deacon Reid wanted to blurt out about all of his surreptitious suspicions, but his wired mouth would not allow him to speak easily.

"Are those men who live upstairs gone?" he asked with a repulsive frown.

"We haven't seen them for a couple of weeks," replied Dennis answering for both of them.

Deacon Reid's face contorted into a taut mask. Responding to what he thought was a grimace of pain Dennis said, "Hey, man, you need to get some rest. Don't starting worrying about Mrs. Caldwell; we'll keep an eye on her." Although the words were meant to be comforting, Deacon Reid felt ill at ease. Oblivious to Deacon Reid's unfinished remarks and strained expression, Dennis disallowed any further mention of concern for Mrs. Caldwell's safety, he said, "We'd better be going, it's getting late."

Louise was troubled by what Deacon Reid had not said. His pain was prevalent, but there was something else troubling him. As they departed, Louise bent over to kiss his forehead, she whispered, "I'll be back tomorrow, we need to talk." Through the aging wrinkles on his face, he displayed his approval of a prospective collaboration between them, as their eyes met in agreement.

28

That evening before Louise fell asleep, she ruminated visiting Deacon Reid on an extended lunch period. She was confident that her boss would not mind. A predicament would only exist if Mrs. Caldwell was present. How would she be able to speak to Deacon Reid freely about her concerns?

Another issue of concern for her was the unquestionable fatigue she was experiencing lately due to her pregnancy. Driven by her curiosity apropos to the men and the history of the bullion, the situation was energizing. She made up in her mind that there was no time for complacency.

Watching Dennis sleep peacefully at her side, she leaned over and kissed him delicately on his cheek. He came home exhausted after working all day. That evening after their return from the hospital, he sat in front of the television to relax but kept dozing off on the couch. Louise urged him to go to bed and as soon as his head touched the pillow, he went out like a light.

)0(

Prior to leaving for work, Louise stopped to visit Mrs. Caldwell. She rang the doorbell and the older woman appeared at the door in a floor length nightgown and robe, looking worn and weary.

"I'm sorry to bother you so early, I hope I didn't wake you," announced Louise.

"Good morning, child. I was just resting in the bed. I've been awake for a while."

"Are you feeling alright?" asked Louise bearing a distressful frown in regard to the older woman's statement and her lethargic-looking condition.

"I'm just a little tired. During the night, I experienced some pains in my chest, so I decided to stay in the bed a little longer before starting my day. You know I have to go to the hospital to see Rufus," she said without giving another thought to her own condition.

"What kind of chest pains?" asked Louise with apprehension. "Are they like heartburn or shortness of breath-related?"

"Lately, I've been having reoccurrences of chest pains after I eat late at night."

"When was the last time you visited a doctor? I remember my grandfather experienced chest pains and a couple of times they radiated down his left arm. He died a few years ago from a heart attack. I don't mean to alarm you, ma'am, but I think you need to be visiting a doctor today instead of Deacon Reid. He'll understand."

"Maybe you're right. I'll give my doctor a call and see if I can come in today."

"That's an excellent idea. I tell you what, how about if I go visit Deacon Reid on my lunch?"

"Thanks, Louise, for your help. Deacon Reid will be glad to see you. Please don't mention to him that I had to go to the doctor. I don't want him worrying about me."

"Sure thing, Mrs. Caldwell, I'll tell him you had some errands to take care of and that you'll see him tomorrow." Louise was pleased with herself for the way she manipulated the situation.

)0(

Deacon Reid was sitting in a chair, staring out of the window, looking at the traffic of people going in and out of the hospital, when Louise arrived.

"Hello, Deacon Reid, how are you feeling today?" she asked as she touched his arm softly before sliding into a chair near him.

"I'll do, Louise. I'm glad you could come."

"Mrs. Caldwell told me to tell you she has some errands to run today, so she'll see you tomorrow."

"Is everything alright?" he asked with a look of anxiety.

"Yes, she'll be here tomorrow," said Louise trying to sound as nonchalant as possible.

"Although it's uncomfortable to talk because of this contraption," said Deacon Reid gesturing to his mouth, "I've got to talk to you. I've got to talk to someone…"

"What's the matter, Deacon Reid? Is something troubling you?"

Louise listened with patience. When she did not understand something Deacon Reid said, he often had to repeat it. He became discouraged when Louise did not understand what he was saying.

"I've been rehashing what happened to me and my fears are getting worse," he said ignoring the pain and difficulty to enunciate.

"Take your time and speak slowly," she encouraged.

He repeated his previous statement regarding his fears. Louise nodded as she strained her ears to understand.

"What do you mean?" she asked.

"I think I know who attacked me."

"Oh, my God! Who?"

"I don't have proof, but I believe it was Flora's other tenants."

"Mark and Paul?"

"Yes, if that's their names," he said somberly.

"How can you be for sure?"

"I can tell a jailbird when I see one. They act shifty and try too hard to blend in. I've worked with many of them," he said obsessively.

"If I tell you that I know for a fact that at least one of them is, you must promise not to tell anyone, until we can sort this out. Okay?"

"I promise, but how do you know?"

Louise explained in detail the chances she had been taking in searching the men's apartment and what she found out about Paul. What she omitted were details about the bullion and the map.

Shocked by her boldness, Deacon Reid said, "You could have gotten caught or hurt or even worse killed or molested by those two." He scolded her for snooping.

"I know, but I had to take the chance, I don't trust them."

"Why? Did they try to do something to you?"

"Mark, the younger one got fresh with me. I warned him to stay away from me."

Deacon Reid displayed his repugnance by sternly staring at her and hanging onto every word. "Did you tell Dennis?"

"No, I couldn't. Dennis would be infuriated and I didn't want him to have a confrontation with him."

"Did Mark say something to you that he shouldn't have?" asked Deacon Reid, his resentment incessantly seeping from him.

"Well yes, but…"

"But what?" His eyes squinted with contempt.

"He touched me on the thigh, but it was an accident."

"What do you mean?"

"He refused to allow me to pass him to go up the stairs to visit Mrs. Caldwell. When he tried to block my path, his knee accidentally touched my leg."

"Are you certain it was an accident?"

"Yeah. Yeah, it was."

Relaxing his guard, Deacon Reid said, "You still can't trust him, please be careful. Try not to be alone with them. What made you search their apartment?"

"I don't feel safe around them and I am concerned for Mrs. Caldwell's welfare."

"So am I. I figure they are conmen that prey on innocent victims."

"Me too," collaborated Louise, realizing she had never thought of them in that fashion. "What are we going to do?" she asked.

"When I tried to express my concerns about them to Flora, she chewed my head off. They don't fool me, though."

"Me neither," added Louise. "What makes you think they were the ones who attacked you?"

Deacon Reid began speaking too fast and she couldn't understand many of his words. After several repetitions of his story, she understood him to say, "We had a nasty encounter when Flora and I came to her house after church. I didn't realize they were living upstairs, so when they were leaving the yard, I gave them a hard time. Flora intervened and they left. I believe they followed me to the liquor store and waited for me to come out."

"Are you certain, it was them?" Louise asked.

"No, I'm not, but think about it, doesn't it make sense? They're up to something and don't want me in their way."

If only I could tell you, contemplated Louise, knowing it would be unwise to confide in him completely.

"There's something else that bothers me," Deacon Reid continued. "When I asked Flora how those men found out about her available apartment, she said that Maurice and Janice, the previous tenants, told them they were moving out. I wanted to confirm this with them, but Flora wouldn't give me their new phone number."

"Why wouldn't she?"

Deacon Reid squirmed a bit before admitting it was an unpleasant topic between him and Mrs. Caldwell.

"She said I was meddling in her business because of my disapproval of the men."

"Why did they move?"

"Didn't Flora tell you?"

"She said they moved out of the state," said Louise focusing on the pupils of his eyes for more of an explanation.

"They began having a stroke of bad luck," replied Deacon Reid.

"What do you mean?" Louise asked, reservedly afraid of what he would say.

"The husband got beat up and robbed."

"I thought Mrs. Caldwell said that she wasn't aware of any crimes like that happening in our neighborhood."

"Louise, the attacks weren't in our neighborhood. Maurice was attacked around his job. His wife was brutally raped one evening after she left her job." Shifting his head, he displayed a sudden omniscient thought.

Deacon Reid conveyed the details of events in the methodical manner of speaking he had adapted to because of the wires that held his mouth together. He nodded his cognition as the pieces of his fragmented puzzle linked themselves together. His words sent chills down Louise's spine as she unconsciously wrapped her arms tightly around her body. Everything made sense to her as well. The men had been planning to get the treasure for a long time and when obstacles got in their way, they systematically removed them. Deacon Reid was their latest victim, which left Mrs. Caldwell, Dennis, and herself. Louise shuddered at the horrid thought of harm trying to find its way to them. With conflicting ambivalence, she resolved there was only so much information she could divulge to Deacon Reid.

In exasperation Deacon Reid said, "Seems to me, those men are directing their intentions at Flora and she's in danger! His eyeballs protruded as he added, "I'm injured and I can't protect her!"

Louise hated having to agree with him, because he did not need anymore worrisome thoughts. She replied, "No, you can't, but Dennis and I can watch over her.

"I don't think so! You're not at home during the day and they're living in the same house with her. They can do something to her and you wouldn't necessarily know it until it was too late."

He was right, but somehow, she had to alleviate his fears since it was not going to do him any good worrying about Mrs. Caldwell while he was in the hospital.

"Please take comfort in knowing that Mrs. Caldwell is here with you nearly everyday. Dennis and I are home in the evening. I promise we'll watch and listen out for her. I'm certain that this is all a coincidence and that we are overreacting," said Louise trying to sound convincing. "Just because Paul has spent time in jail, doesn't mean that he hadn't reformed. He does carry himself like a gentleman."

"Yep, a con artist would! Don't tell me you're changing your attitude toward those men." He gawked at her in disgust. "I see what you're trying to do and it won't work, young lady. There's nothing you can do or say that will convince me that those men are on the straight and narrow!" His voice cracked as he slashed out at Louise causing her to look at him with penance. "You didn't come here to calm my fears regarding those men. You came because you don't trust them. Now, stop playing games with me!"

"You're right, but…"

"Louise, don't patronize me! Help me find a solution! My Flora isn't safe!"

Together the pair formulated a plan that was satisfactory to both of them, one that would not arouse the attention of Mrs. Caldwell.

29

"I can hardly wait until we get home," said Mark, looking out the window of the car at nothing in particular. Finishing their tour of duty, which consisted of cleaning and assisting with unloading the railcars, the men drove from the rail yard. Leaving behind them were rows of railroad tracks filled with multitude freight cars waiting to be loaded and unloaded, while other cars waited to be shipped and stored. There was plenty of activity with workers chatting while rerouting cars to different tracks and directing the flow of traffic. On one end of the yard, trailers previously removed from freight trucks were hoisted up into the air onto flat beds so they could ride piggy back on the railroad tracks.

Paul and Mark were tired and were looking forward to time off.

"Toss you for the shower first," said Mark. A quarter twirled up in the air, slightly touching the roof of the car.

"Heads or tails?" he asked Paul after catching it and placing it on the back of his hand.

"Tails," said Paul.

Both men looked as Mark removed his hand. "*Haennnnn! Haennnnn!* I get to shower first," laughed Mark, bobbing his head up and down to unheard music in his head.

Exacerbated by his cockiness, Paul played it off, he responded, "That's okay by me. I'll drop you off at home, then I'll stop at the barbershop, and go to the grocery store."

"I need a haircut too. Why can't you wait on me?"

"Make up your mind, shower, or haircut."

"Okay you can shower first, we'll go to the store, and then we both can get shaves and haircuts. I'll shower later," Mark resolved.

"Let's stop at the barber's first, grocery store, and then home in that order," advised Paul.

"Okay, but when we get home, I'm showering first," said Mark with satisfaction.

"No, you aren't, you just said that I could shower first."

They bickered back and forth until Mark conceded.

Paul knew how to manipulate Mark by perpetrating a deception and found pleasure in doing so. Mark would rush through his shower and would probably disappear for the evening while Paul was still bathing. As a safeguard, it was important for Paul to keep tabs on him, since he was not trustworthy enough to stay out of trouble on his own. There was plenty of work to do, and he could not afford for Mark to get out of control or do anything that would land him back in jail.

Meticulous about his body, Paul knew that Mark did not care one way or another about his. Through his tutelage, he insisted that Mark maintain good hygiene, otherwise, he would not have continued their partnership. If Mark had his way, he would splash a few dabs of water on himself, back it with some cheap cologne, and hit the street in search of a good time. Traveling with Paul, Mark found that his fair looks and cleanliness attracted more women, elevating him to heights he quickly learned to enjoy.

Mark tried to follow in Paul's footsteps, but there were several years' difference in their ages, and he had different tastes than Paul. His sexual satisfaction took priority, and besides, he loved his brusque treatment of women during sex. If they were exceptionally extraordinary, he only roughed them up a little. Fervently, he enjoyed the sounds of their screams of pain. Every now and then, he encountered a woman who actually enjoyed it. One of his coupling partners was Molly. Not only did she enjoy his rough treatment, but she also enjoyed administrating it. Their last encounter left his back raw from whip lashings, and he could not lean against anything for a week. This brought him to the decision that he did not like being at the receiving end.

When he was with Paul, he had to behave himself, or else Paul would beat the crap out of him. Paul adored women and treated them with kindness and respect. Contrarily, Mark did not think of women in that manner. They were something he used for his entertainment, otherwise, they were of no use to him. Depending upon Mark's mood, he would travel with or without Paul. Tonight, he wanted his independence. After being on the road for sixteen days, he earned it.

Taunted by his desire to seduce Louise, Mark could not get her out of his mind. For weeks, he schemed on snatching her when she entered the yard or grabbing her while she worked in it, or possibly following her to or from her job and pulling her into an alley. Moreover, Louise needed slapping around a bit because she acted too high and mighty for a nigger. He promised himself to take her down a notch or two. Caution was necessary because if she recognized him it would interfere with Paul's plan. But then again, what satisfaction would he get if she did not know who he was? He had not worked out the details of her demise, but he continued to fantasize about it. Until he could come up with a satisfactory plan, he had to fulfill his desires elsewhere.

)0(

On the night, that Deacon Reid was missing, in the early hours of the morning, Paul and Mark returned home. The neighborhood and streets were quiet. As their lone vehicle turned the corner onto the deserted street, all the lights were out on the block except at Mrs. Caldwell's house. After their evening meal and a few drinks at a bar a few miles away, the men returned home and could hear through Mrs. Caldwell's front door that she was still entertaining Deacon Reid. After giving the matter some consideration, Paul decided that they should go back to their car and wait for him to leave.

In the dark, the men followed their unsuspecting prey to the liquor store and lain in wait for him. Upon returning to his car, they pulled him into the darkened cove of the entrance to a store. Deacon Reid was not a frail man and could have warded off the average would be attacker, if there had been only one assailant, but there were two of them. Paul grabbed him viciously from behind by his neck, while Mark disguised by a ski mask repeatedly jabbed his fists into his rib cage. During the struggle, the bag with the liquor in it fell to the ground and the glass broke, spilling its contents onto the pavement. As Deacon Reid tried to break the hold around his neck, he managed to slam his fist into Mark's face. In doing so, he broke his hand. He was bashed in the back of his head with something hard, his knees buckled, and his body crumbled to the ground. The men raced away, but Mark returned, searched though his pockets, and procured his wallet. As he extracted the little money from the wallet, he muttered in disgust, "He could have had more money, what a waste." Discarding the wallet, he threw it in the back of their car where it tumbled to the floor underneath the seat.

Paul smugly announced, "I didn't need another person interfering with my plans. What we've done is eliminate another prospective problem. That old man will be laid up for at least a month and by then we should have found the bullion."

"That old dude put up a struggle. He deserved what he got after hitting me in the eye. *Haennnnn!*" said Mark. When he went to look at his face in the bathroom mirror, he replied, "Damn! Look at what that arrogant ass bastard did to my face! How am I going to cover up a black eye and these bruises?"

"We're leaving on the train the day after tomorrow. Until then you'll have to lay low in the house. When we leave, wear your sunglasses, and don't worry about the rest," advised Paul with assurance.

30

Now that the men were off the road, the time had come for them to take action on Iroquois Street. With a seven day layover, Paul reconciled that they had to find the bullion. Too much interference with his plans had already occurred. The latest obstacle was getting rid of the old man, and still there were three other contenders. The way he saw it, Mrs. Caldwell was not a problem, but having to confront the country hick and his feisty wife was not something he looked forward to dealing with. Dennis seemed strong enough to beat him and Mark into mush. If only Mrs. Caldwell had not rented the coach house to them, his plans would have been less complicated. Mesmerized by the wife, Mark could not keep his eyes or thoughts off of her, and that was another potential problem.

Optimistic about finding the bullion, Paul realized after locating it, the immediate necessity for them to disappear. When he provided employment information to Mrs. Caldwell and repeated it to the Clark couple, he and Mark lied about being inspectors for the railroad company. He knew it was risky even stating that they worked for the railroad company, but when they initially met with Mrs. Caldwell, Mark blurted out the information before he could say otherwise. There was an underlying fear of being caught, but that was the chance he would have to take. With so much planning, he found that the mental preparation was exhausting.

As far as Paul was concerned, it was not whether or not they would find the bullion, but when they would find it. His confidence gave him a pseudo belief that he was on the right track, and normally, his hunches did not steer him too far afield. After locating the bullion, he would have enough money to open up his own restaurant, using one of the city's top chefs. *Which chef can I steal?* he asked himself. This time he would be smarter, he would be on easy street, and did not foresee anymore con games in his future. He could become one of the fine upstanding members of society, putting his roguish past behind him.

Unable to picture Mark in his future, he would have to rid himself of him at some point. Paul was indecisive about how he would do it, since there was no need to sustain a relationship with him. Pragmatically, Paul knew with Mark's history, he would raise enough havoc, which would land him back in jail in no time.

)0(

"Mark, we're going to step up our search for the bullion," said Paul.

"I thought you said we had plenty of time on our hands. What's the big rush?"

"Dumpy, if you haven't noticed, more and more players are becoming involved, we don't need anymore interferences. I want you to crawl under this house in search of the bullion."

Mark started to rebut forcefully, but the way Paul gawked at him made him reconsider.

"What are you going to be doing, while I'm getting dirty?" he asked, cowering by putting some distance between them.

"I'm going to get into Mrs. Caldwell's apartment, even if I have to break a window to gain access to it, to search for the bullion. I probably won't find it there and if that's the case, I'm going to take the door off the hinges to the coach house. The bullion has got to be under us or somewhere in the coach house. That's the only thing that makes sense."

"You didn't have any luck jimmying the locks. What makes you think you can take a door off its hinges? *Haennnnn! Haennnnn!*" said Mark with his annoying snicker."

"Shut the fuck up! For your information I ran into a locksmith and he told me how to do it."

"Telling you and you actually doing it *ain't* the same thing. *Haennnnn!*" replied Mark.

"Don't worry, I'll be prepared when the time is right," said Paul, confident that he could conquer the door.

)0(

After bathing, unobtrusively Mark tried to ease out of the apartment. When his hand touched the doorknob to open the backdoor, Paul appeared out of nowhere standing so close to him that he could feel his breath on the back of his neck. Mark turned toward him revealing his set of pearly whites. He said, "I'm on my way out, I'll see you later. *Haennnnn!*" The men were almost equal in height. Paul placed his hand on top of Mark's and forcedly dug his fingernails into the back of Mark's hand, prying it from the doorknob. Mark snatched his hand free, rubbing it to soothe the pain.

"What did you do that for?" he asked stunned by Paul's use of force.

"I thought we'd go to dinner together, find some broads, and then do what comes naturally," said Paul shrewdly.

"Huh?"

"Huh what?" replied Paul. "Is there something wrong with your hearing?"

"*Naw*, man, but I'd rather hang out alone tonight. I've been with you for over two weeks. I'm *figurin'* we need some space between us. So if you don't mind, I'm going out by myself tonight. *Haennnnn!*"

"You figured wrong, buddy! We're hanging out together tonight and every other night, until we finish doing what we came to accomplish!" ordered Paul. His tone was nonnegotiable. "You'll have plenty of time to get into mischief after we finish this job. Do you understand?"

The men were facing each other. Paul stood steadfast at Mark's chest, geared up to fight against any resistance. "*Naw* man, I'm going out!" slashed Mark, shouting in an effort to display his unwavering decision to leave. He shoved Paul away from him and started to open the door. Paul's arms encircled Mark's chest from behind and he threw him on the floor.

"Over my dead body!" replied Paul, huffing and puffing. With all his strength, Mark pushed his legs against the wall and kicked himself free from Paul's hold. Mark turned and aimed his fist at Paul's face, but Paul dodged to the left. Paul issued a counterblow aimed at the center of Mark's face. The punch landed on Mark's nose, causing blood to splatter and trickle down on his mouth and chin. Mark saw stars upon impact and wiped the blood from his face with the back of his hand. He roared and swung wildly, trying to get the best of Paul, anticipating that his youthfulness would aid him against Paul's experience and strength.

Mark shook his head in an attempt to clear it and gain control of the situation. Both men lunged at each other in an undisciplined fight, swinging arms and kicking feet. Paul kicked Mark in his groin as hard as he could and that halted Mark's resistance. "*Ow, ow!*" cried Mark. "*Fuckin'* asshole, you fight dirty! You've messed me up! *Ahhhh!*" he abhorrently bellowed, moaning from spasms of pain. His capitulation left him rolled up in a ball on the floor. Feeling sorry for his unworthy opponent, Paul extended his hand to help him up from the floor. With acrimony, Mark jerked away from him refusing his assistance. "Get the fuck away from me!" he retorted with venom.

With a raise of his eyebrows, Paul signified his satisfaction in preventing Mark from leaving. Mark lied on the floor, immobile. Several moments passed before he was able to move. Belligerently cursing while holding his crotch, he retreated slowly to his bedroom, eased onto the bed, and wallowed in pain.

31

After their confrontation, Paul went to a tavern to order a drink and calm himself. Although he won the best of Mark, his body ached, and a drink helped to nurse the pain. Paul stayed in shape by exercising, a habit he started in prison. Infrequently, he found himself in a bind, where he needed to ward off an opponent, therefore, the exercise paid off. Every now and then, he had to put Mark in his place. There was a fifteen year difference in their ages, but Paul always seemed to know how to undermine him.

Cogitating over Mark, Paul deemed that he was not too perverse, if you could tolerate his antics. Quite often, he was perceptive and handled himself well in difficult situations. He grew up in an abusive home where his father drank excessively and would beat on him, his mother, and siblings. Attempting not to be like his father, Mark controlled his drinking. His rough treatment of women, which often turned brutal during sex, was a correlation to his father's actions.

At the bar Paul sat next to two attractive women who were talking incessantly about a number of things, one of which he deciphered was money problems. One woman was an office clerk, who listened with patience, while her friend, a waitress complained about a customer who mistreated her by being rude and shouting obscenities at her, when she did not serve him fast enough. Paul joined in the conversation by suggesting how she could have handled the situation better.

"How could I have, after he humiliated me in front of everyone?" she asked in exasperation.

"You could have offered to sit on his lap and feed him for free," said Paul.

"With or without *skimpies?*" she asked as the whole group cackled.

This opened the door for Paul, and he offered to buy them drinks. He was attracted to the waitress, probably because they had more in common since they worked in the restaurant industry. By womanizing, Paul expertly manipulated the conversation, while continually purchasing their drinks.

Using a straightforward approach, as the evening progressed Paul explained that he was out for a good time. He suggested ordering dinners for takeout and getting some alcohol, meaning he wanted the full gambit of the wining, dining, and then some. He further explained that his grown son, Mark would be involved and that he had been in a recent accident and would probably be unable to participate in any heavy petting. He felt that he could receive the benefits of being lavished with intimate kisses. After flashing his money as he paid for the drinks, he promised to compensate the women for their time. With amusement, Paul watched as the slightly inebriated women discussed his proposition among themselves. They accepted his offer and followed him home in the office clerk's automobile.

)0(

The sound of laughter and music filtered through the apartment, greeting Mark when he woke up. Paul was entertaining a couple of women who were laughing about something he said. After delicately touching his crotch, Mark cringed, but went to relieve himself in the bathroom. In front of the mirror on the door, he dropped his trousers allowing them to crumble around his ankles so he could examine himself. His left thigh was black and blue and his private parts throbbed from pain. As far as any intimate performance, he would be out of commission for a while. Directing his antagonism toward Paul for causing him pain and preventing him from enjoying himself, he cursed poignantly. *Why are there two women in our apartment? Are they going to bed with Paul? At asshole's age, that's a joke,* chuckled Mark with envy. With his poor member out of action, all he would be able to do was watch, if Paul allowed that.

In the mirror of the medicine cabinet, he ran one hand over his face to examine it. It was puffy and bruised with dried blood around his nostrils. He washed his face to remove the traces of blood and ran water over his comb to straighten his hair. The smell of food beckoned him from the bathroom. At the entrance to the dimly lit living room, he stood looking upon its inhabitants, before all heads turned toward him.

With the charisma of a wealthy diplomat Paul extended his hand, he said, "Jeanne and Mary Ann, meet my son, Mark." After the introductions he added, "Mark, you're welcome to join us. There's plenty of food and beer here. Dig in my boy."

Paul's generous reception was sickening. Mark directed a smile toward the women, but presented Paul with a scornful glower. Displaying a jovial façade, Paul resumed his conversation with the women he said, "Now ladies as I was saying…"

Seating himself on the sofa, next to the women, Mark dug into the food and popped the cap off of a bottle of beer. Sloughing off his revulsion of Paul with the downing of a couple of beers, Mark chose not to be a spoilsport. He found enjoyment in slow dancing and cuddling, which he took full advantage of by constantly snuggling his head in between the well endowed bosom of the office clerk. She giggled, "You naughty boy," after which he would make a nose dive, repeating the action. Later in the evening, he explained awkwardly to the clerk that he was somewhat incapacitated. Finding that it did not matter to her, he was able to receive undulating satisfaction from her tender loving kisses, which made him happier than a hog in slop.

)0(

While Louise finished washing the dishes from their supper, she looked out of the kitchen window toward the back of the second floor of Mrs. Caldwell's house. Keeping tabs on the men's apartment was a daily routine. This was part of the pact that she and Deacon Reid made amongst themselves the day she visited him by herself at the hospital. Louise would check on Mrs. Caldwell each morning prior to departing for work, as well as studying the house and observing the comings and goings of the men, the best she could from her house. Deacon Reid would detain her all afternoon at the hospital so she would arrive home about the same time in the evening as the young Clarks. Additionally, he would call her every night before going to sleep. Deacon Reid and Louise reconciled that going to the police would be unproductive, without sufficient evidence linking the conmen to Deacon Reid's attack. Louise recognized the fact that Dennis would be furious with her for not collaborating with him, but she felt he was not ready to accept that the evil men were dangerous and were seeking the bullion.

When she looked up at the second floor and saw lights on in the kitchen and Mark's bedroom, she knew the men had returned. All the peacefulness everyone had been experiencing was about to dissipate. *Why couldn't they have been in a train derailment and died,* she deliberated, only to feel guilty for her thoughts. *Why did they have to come back?* She knew the answer to that question, better than anyone else did.

)0(

Mrs. Caldwell did not discover that the men were home until late in the evening when she heard them arrive on the front porch. There was plenty of giggling from women, which made her listen at her door. Someone stumbled on the stairs and Paul made a racy comment about her tush, when he evidently caught one of the women in his arms. Shortly after that, music from a radio began playing and she felt the vibrations from their dancing through her ceiling. She found amusement in their merriment and yearned to dance with Deacon Reid. This was the first time the men had women in their apartment that she was aware of, and she felt it was quite appropriate. Matter-of-fact, she felt safer with the men in the house.

)0(

The women had departed several hours before Paul finally got up for the day. He was downing a sip of coffee and thumbing through yesterday's newspaper, when he heard the downstairs front door slammed. Mrs. Caldwell was leaving out. Quickly, he raised a window in the living room and shouted out for her to wait for him to come down. She nodded agreeably. Taking a couple of swigs of mouthwash, he joined her by the gate. His unbuttoned shirt flew open exposing the hair on his chest.

"Hello, Flora, dear, you look charming, as always," he said in seductive tone that sent a chill through her, especially after spying his sinewy chest.

He handed her the rent money, after which she said, "Thank you, Paul. I'd better take this in the house and make out a receipt for you."

"Oh, you can give it to me later."

"That's alright, I don't want to carry extra money around."

Paul followed her up the stairs and stood behind her while she opened her door. He said, "We got back yesterday afternoon."

"I gathered as much, after hearing music last night."

"I hope we weren't too loud and didn't disturb you since we were entertaining guests."

"No, not at all. I could tell you were having fun. You deserved it after your long trip."

"You're right about that," chuckled Paul thoughtfully playing with his mustache. "My boy is still asleep."

Paul followed her into the dining room.

"Please have a seat," she offered motioning to a chair. "Would you care for some coffee or tea?"

"No thanks, I've interrupted you enough already."

His eyes followed her as she pulled her receipt book out of a drawer of the credenza. While Mrs. Caldwell sat down and started writing, he asked, "Where are you off to on such a fine day?"

"I'm on my way to the hospital to visit my friend, Rufus. You met him. He had a terrible run in with some muggers two weeks ago."

"Oh, what happened?" asked Paul appearing legitimately concerned.

In detail, Mrs. Caldwell explained about Deacon Reid's tragedy and that she visited him every afternoon in the hospital. "Deacon Reid will be getting out of the hospital soon and he will be coming to live with me, so I can nurse him back to health."

Displeased with her report, he concealed his disapproval with a forced smile. While Mrs. Caldwell spoke, he patted his foot impatiently, wanting her to hurry on her way. "I'm sorry your friend ran into foul play, if there's anything we can do to help you, please let me know. How long do you normally stay at the hospital?" he asked unobtrusively. "Perhaps Mark and I can come by to visit," he continued, careful in his articulation so she would not notice his inquisition.

"I normally stay until supper time."

"If I don't see you today, we'll try to make it tomorrow."

"That's so kind of you, but you don't have to do that. You really don't know him, she said nervously speaking fast. "I'm glad you're back. Take it easy and enjoy your time at home."

Hoping she had discouraged Paul from going to the hospital, Mrs. Caldwell knew that Deacon Reid would have a fit if either of the men showed up there. Every time she left him, he warned her to be careful and she knew that his warnings were directed toward the men, but for the life of her, she could not understand the rationale for it. After all, she was not that naive that she could not tell if an individual's intentions were sinister or not.

32

Heeding Louise's advice, Mrs. Caldwell made an appointment to see her physician the same day. After taking a battery of tests, her doctor advised her that the chest pains she was experiencing were in association to her heart. He prescribed heart and blood pressure medications informing her to take it easy, avoid stressful situations when possible, and eat healthy by watching her sodium and fried food intake. She assured him she would and he advised her that she had nothing to worry about and would live for several more years without any problems.

)0(

Mrs. Caldwell spent time cleaning one of her spare bedrooms for Deacon Reid. Trying not to make the room too frilly, she chose curtains with a line pattern, something masculine that she felt he would appreciate. Occasionally, she stopped by his apartment to tidy it up and take him his mail. Mrs. Caldwell had not mentioned to him she wanted him to move in permanently, but was saving this conversation for her afternoon visit. They could combine their resources and live comfortably together.

Yearning to work out some of the details as soon as possible, she decided this was also the perfect day to confess her love for him; something she knew he had been waiting to hear from her for a long time. This newfound declaration made her feel like a giddy teenager, bursting to release stacked up emotions from her denial of a relationship that overflowed with promise. It was a suffocating, but good feeling that seemed to rest profoundly upon her chest, constantly reminding her it was there and making her lightheaded with happiness. This euphoric state was one of contentment, an inhibited mature feeling untainted by misleading falsehoods. In every leisure moment, her thoughts were of Rufus, not as a friend or companion, but more as a partner to love, the missing element in her life. *This woman has found herself a man to love, a real live man.* She chuckled at her naughty thoughts.

Initially arbitrating that she was too old for such nonsense as love and having an intimate companion, she immediately saw the error of her judgment. *You are old, when you cannot get around anymore on your own and can no longer do for yourself. You are old, when you are weak, tired, and have a nameless list of ailments with hordes of medication you cannot pronounce.* Except for her recent doctor's visit, she had always been healthy, therefore, she did not fall into her definition of old, nor did she feel old. *I've got many more years ahead of me. I'm going to have a ball with Rufus and make up for lost time,* she surmised. *The time I spent mourning for my dear Percy is over. It's time for the living and I've got plenty to make up for. Percy, I know you'd want me to be happy and I'd want the same for you,* she convinced herself. The clarity of seeing herself in a new life was exciting.

Rufus was her future now and together they would plan it wisely. At her age, few people got the chance to be blissfully in love and here was her big opportunity. Rufus had been by her side for several years, and not until recently did she comprehend the meaning of true friendship and her feelings for him. She was not going to waste anymore precious time on foolish thoughts.

Her attitude regarding the accomplishments she made on her own and not sharing them with him ingratiatingly dissolved. If Deacon Reid brought nothing to the table, it was inconsequential, because his devotion to her would suffice. She tried to think of some of his bad habits and was only able to come up with him sucking his teeth after he ate in an effort to clean them. Flora kept a supply of toothpicks wrapped in tissue handy and when he started this annoying practice, she offered him one so he could quietly pick his teeth. Other than that, he was the man meant for her. There was one other thing that irritated her. His refusal to travel with her to visit her children, but was that because they were not bound by matrimony as husband and wife? She had never entertained that thought. *He is a wonderful man, and I'm thankful to have him. After all these years, what took you so long, you foolish woman?*

)0(

"You look awfully pretty today, Flora," said Deacon Reid as she entered his room wearing a smart looking blue dress that fit neatly over her proportioned body.

Blushing and looking down at her shoes, she said, "Thanks, Rufus. How are you today?"

He reported that his ribs were well on their way to healing properly. He had a physical therapy session and would have to continue therapy for a few weeks. "The young doc told me that I can be released from the hospital in a few days," he volunteered with enthusiasm. As he spoke slowly, she became uncomfortably warm inside, so much so that she began fanning herself with her visitor's pass.

"Are you feeling alright?" he wanted to know.

"I'm fine," she replied glimmering with pleasure from the nearness of him. Anxiously, she shifted from side to side, she said, "Rufus, that's wonderful news. When will they remove the wiring from your mouth?"

"A few more weeks and I'll practically be my old self again. Then I can kiss my gal properly if she'll let me."

"And just who might that be?" she asked.

"Come over here woman and give me a hug," he demanded widening his arms to receive her. "You're one of the most *stubborniest* people I know. I love you, Flora. Don't you know that? I've felt this way ever since your Percy died. Haven't I been the one to take care of you and comfort you? How could you not know the way I feel about you?"

"Rufus, I love you, too. I've been a silly old woman. It took this to happen for me to see how much you mean to me."

Deacon Reid's smile was as broad as a church woman's butt. His heart fluttered with happiness.

"When I get back on my feet, will you marry me?" he asked gazing into her eyes.

"Yes!" she responded without any hesitation, displaying her sincerity by climbing onto the bed and giving him a hug.

"Gentle, gentle now!" he warned, splinting his rib cage. He stroked her hair, while he held her.

Deacon Reid asked her to marry him before she had the opportunity to profess her undying affection for him. Mrs. Caldwell guessed he always knew her true feelings, but it was important that he heard her declaration of affection.

"Rufus, I have been a contrary old woman who thought that I didn't need another man in my life. I've been so iron-willed in my beliefs that I thought I could make it on my own without any help from you. The reality of it all is that I didn't do anything on my own. After Percy died, you were always there to guide me. I probably wouldn't have bought my house, using the second floor for income if you hadn't advised me to do so. You were that unconscious voice that counseled me to invest my money wisely, making me think it was my own decision. When my house needed repairs, if you didn't fix it, you told me where to go to get it done. I've spent wasteful time thinking I was so self-sufficient, when it was you, always in my corner. Stupidly, I denied your devotion, thinking I didn't need you as a permanent fixture in my life. Forgive me for all the times I refused to allow you to get close to me. I know I've made you suffer. How you have put up with me this long is a pure puzzlement!"

Deacon Reid smiled as she spoke. He knew this woman of his was a proud and independent person. He replied, "Flora, you have always been my gal, now hush. There's nothing for me to forgive because we have always had each other. We're just *gonna* start out with a different approach."

They kissed softly and held hands.

"When you get out of here you're moving in with me," she declared with watery eyes.

He forced himself to hold back his own tears.

Mrs. Caldwell and Deacon Reid spent their time together professing their true feelings and preparing for their future. They decided to start packing up his belongings, sorting out the items to keep, and what to sale or give away. Their planning kept them busy through dinnertime and one of the thoughtful nurses obtained a dinner tray for Mrs. Caldwell.

"Flora, after we get married I want to go on a honeymoon to Europe or a cruise to a Caribbean island," Deacon Reid announced.

Astonished by his statement, she looked at him in shock. "Where did you get such ideas, Rufus?"

"I've always wanted to go, but the time never seemed right. I can't think of a better reason than a honeymoon," he replied seriously. "I've done nothing but save my money through the years, and I don't intend on dying and leaving it behind."

She sat there dumbfounded with her mouth wide open, a bug could have flown in it. "I had no idea that you were in the position to do anything like that," she proclaimed marveling because of her misconceptions about him.

"There are a lot of things you don't know about me, Flora, but in time you will," he said, smiling as he grasped her hand to squeeze it.

He named several of the places he wanted to visit, places that she never heard of. He spoke of the captivating islands in Hawaii and the Philippines, and the different customs that some of the natives kept. This was just the beginning of the stories he intended to share with her. His exhilaration made him feel pungent enough to heal himself swiftly so he could plunge into a new vivacious life with her.

After Mrs. Caldwell left, Deacon Reid reminisced about the years he spent yearning for this woman who refused to acknowledge him as nothing more than a mere friend. He had resigned himself to accept their relationship on Flora's terms. Due to his long-lasting determination to pursue the woman who held his heart captive, a life with her would turn into gratifying fruition. No longer did he see himself as a fragment of a man who pitied himself for becoming old and weak, but a whole one, ready to conquer the next phase of his life.

33

After paying rent to Mrs. Caldwell, Paul climbed up the stairs to his apartment. With great urgency, he roused Mark from his bed. Mark spent the day scrounging around underneath Mrs. Caldwell's house in search of the bullion with the aid of a shovel, iron rod, and pick. The confinement of working in a small space made him measly uncomfortable. Combating spider webs, some with spiders, ants, and other creepy crawlers, caused him to fidget constantly in an effort to rid himself of them. Keeping his aggravations at bay, he psyched himself up to believe that the culmination of the job would lead him to riches beyond his imagination.

He knew that his cohort and often mentor did not think he was intelligent enough to exist on his own without getting into trouble, but he would prove his merit to him. With his share of the money after the disposal of the bullion, his intentions were to buy a spanking new red tow truck and a house with a yard like old lady Caldwell's to live in. Of course, he would require the services of a maid to keep the place orderly for him, some elderly woman that needed to make some extra money. That should suffice, demonstrating to Paul that he possessed some compassion for women. Wretchedly sweaty and dirty, he cursed grudgingly under his breath while relentlessly performing his task.

While Mark was digging, Paul checked to see if by any chance Mrs. Caldwell forgot to lock her front door. Any tampering he did with the door was noticeable from the street and each of her next door neighbors. He went down the back stairs and jiggled Mrs. Caldwell's backdoor. As he suspected, it was also locked. Without giving anymore thought to it, he focused on the three windows, hoping to gain entry through one of them. Starting with the back-room window, he took his crowbar and slipped it under one end of the windowsill. Pushing downward on the crowbar, he struggled to lift the window. The window remained in place, but the crowbar slipped out from the window heading for the center of his head. With quick impulses, he moved his head to the side, in just enough time to avoid smacking himself in the face. Tersely he cursed. Repositioning the crowbar underneath the middle section of the windowsill, he leaned against the crowbar with his body so that it would not slip out. He tried to raise the window, but it refused to budge. Changing positions, by sliding the crowbar over to the far side, with more exertion, he struggled to pry the window up. It resulted in another unproductive effort.

Immediately, he went to the pair of kitchen windows and attempted the same procedure on the first window. Finding it locked from within, his attempts were ineffective. With resolve, he moved over to the last window. He slid the crowbar under the center of the windowsill, pushed down on the crowbar and there was movement. *My lucky day!* he declared energetically. Paul slid the crowbar toward the opposite end of the window, and it moved upward effortlessly.

Tossing the crowbar on the floor of the porch, Paul had his ingress to enter into Mrs. Caldwell's kitchen. Her apartment was set up in the same manner as his, except there was a third bedroom. Scrupulously, he went through the apartment without finding any evidence of the bullion. Paul exited her apartment the same way he entered, mindfully lowering the window. Proud of himself for masterfully gaining entry into Mrs. Caldwell's house, he acquired the pseudo sense of confidence that he could conquer the doors to the coach house. Celebrating his victory, he took a short break by running upstairs to his apartment to smoke a quick cigarette and to relieve himself before tackling his next project.

)0(

Paul set forth to the business of removing the hinges from the door of the coach house. With a hammer and screwdriver in each hand, he was prepared to pry the hinges up and out of place. Baffled, he stood in front of the doors to the coach house looking for hinges that were not visible. Shaking his head as if developing a form of palsy, he cringed at his ignorance for not realizing that the hinges would be on the other side of the door to prevent an intruder from tampering with them. *How stupid can you get!* he declared, annoyed with himself for his obtuseness. In his exasperation for finding himself in this ludicrous predicament, he kicked the doors and released a lurid curse. Quickly, regaining control of his senses, he reminded himself of the importance of not attracting any unnecessary attention in order to complete his mission. In reconciliation, his only recourse for entering the coach house was to break out a window.

)0(

After his second day of *gawd*-awful digging underneath the house, Mark proclaimed in desolation, "There *ain't* no goddamn gold and silver bars here or anywhere on this shit ass property! We're wasting our time! What would make you ever think that some old rich dude would die and leave it for someone else to find? I bet he sold it or got rid of it long ago!"

"I disagree with you," said Paul shaking his head. "I believe it's here, we just have to find it," he proclaimed with undoubted conviction. "Come help me get into the coach house!"

Carrying a large burlap bag full of the tools they needed, without reservation of being seen, Paul led the way, with Mark close behind him. Paul paused momentarily to snatch a towel hanging on a line from Mrs. Caldwell's laundry. He wrapped it around his hand with the intention of using it as a buffer to break a back window to Louise and Dennis' house.

After the glass shattered, they extracted some of the jagged pieces before Paul said to Mark, "Climb in!" Without any hesitation, Mark climbed through the window with simplicity, entering the couple's living room. He looked around the room, spotting the TV/Hi-fi unit, resolving it met with his approval and noting that he would steal it, if given the opportunity. Proceeding to the door in the kitchen, he unlocked it, allowing Paul to enter.

)0(

Deferring from her regular routine of going to the hospital, Mrs. Caldwell went shopping to get a few things from the grocery store. Advancing into her yard, she heard glass breaking. Rushing to open her door and placing her parcels on the kitchen table, she exited the backdoor to investigate. Upon approaching the coach house, she heard loud knocking evolving from its interior and observed that a door was wide open. "Louise, Dennis, *helloooo?*" she called out. "Is everything okay in there?" Normally, the young couple was not home during the day. Louise had already stopped by to check on her before she departed for work. Mrs. Caldwell ventured inside the house. From the kitchen, she saw Paul tapping on the wall in the living room.

"Paul, what are you doing in here? she shouted over his tapping.

He grunted. Perturbed for being discovered, he stopped what he was doing. Tightening the hold on the hammer in his hand, he replied, "Searching for a hidden treasure Flora. I bet you didn't know you were sitting on a gold mine."

"What are you talking about?"

"Mark and I discovered a while ago that there are bullions of gold and silver here somewhere."

"You must be out of your mind. This property was vacant for years before I bought it," Mrs. Caldwell stood with her arms folded across her chest.

"I'm going to have to ask you to leave."

"I'm sorry, Flora, but you don't have any say in what I'm doing. Matter-of-fact I'm sorry you have interrupted me."

Mark appeared from the back of the house. "Tie her up in a chair in the kitchen and make sure your gag her mouth," Paul instructed him.

"*Haennnnn*! Sure boss! Where is the rope?"

"Look in the bag over there on the floor."

Mrs. Caldwell ran to the door but Mark quickly caught up with her.

"Help! Somebody please help me! I'm being robbed!" shouted the elderly woman swinging her arms wildly.

"Shut her up!" said Paul. He ran over to help Mark subdue her.

Mark was holding a crowbar in his hand. He swung it at Mrs. Caldwell and it struck her on the side of her head, knocking her to the floor. Blood gushed from her head. Mark stood over her in assessment of his handiwork. There were traces of Mrs. Caldwell's blood on the crowbar.

"Good job," said Paul patting him on his back. "We better get her out of sight. Help me move the old broad in the living room.

Lying helplessly across the threshold, Mrs. Caldwell moaned from excruciating pain. Like a sack of potatoes, she felt her body being dragged by both arms, across the floor. "Paul, help me," she pleaded weakly, hoping he would display some form of mercy and provide her with the attention she seriously required. She didn't know what she had been struck with, but knew Mark was the one that hit her. When Paul and Mark dumped her in the living room between the sofa and cocktail table, she was cognitive of the injustices done to her. Menacing pain prevented her from doing anything about it. Conclusively, she realized the validity of Rufus' suspicions concerning the men and how incredulously naive she had been.

"Four down and two more to go, if necessary," mocked Mark.

Mrs. Caldwell wondered what he meant. She parroted his words, "Four down, what do you mean," she asked feebly.

"Shut up old lady! I really liked you, but now you're in the way. You just had to keep on getting new tenants," said Mark.

Paul turned his back and returned to tapping on the wall. Mark's tactics were to torment his victims. He added, "That boyfriend of yours got what he deserved, a true ass kicking from us."

"Get back to work, time is of the essential," warned Paul.

Now, Mrs. Caldwell realized that the men were responsible for the attacks on her former tenants. She only hoped that somehow Louise and Dennis could save her and not get hurt in the process. In extreme pain, she could do no more than lie still on the uncomfortable hard floor. *I must wait for an opportunity to get help,* Mrs. Caldwell planned.

Searching each room, the men looked for signs of aberrations by inspecting and tapping on the floor and walls. They scrutinized the house, careful not to omit the closets and pantry in the kitchen. In the kitchen Paul ordered Mark, "Climb up there and see what you can find," pointing to the crawl space in the ceiling of the pantry.

Paul hoisted Mark up by allowing him to jump up on the inside of his interlocked hands. Mark climbed onto the top shelf touching the neatly folded blanket that concealed Dennis' fully loaded shotgun. Pushing the door open so that he could crawl into the small attic space, he used the shelf with the blanket for leverage. His foot moved the blanket toward the edge of the shelf. "Guess I should be use to this shit! Always doing the dirty work! *Haennnnn!*" he defiantly mumbled down to Paul. On his belly, he crept across the rafters of the limited space, engulfed in spider webs, mouse droppings, and musty old dirt that accumulated over the years, probably since the construction of the coach house. "*Fuckin'* bastard always making me do all the damn work!" Mark cursed underneath his breath as he conducted warfare with spider webs.

After several minutes of listening to Mark glide across the ceiling, Paul shouted, "Tell me something, damn it! Do you see anything up there?"

"Hell no! I'll be down in a minute!"

Paul helped Mark down from the crawl space by holding his legs. Staggering while he tried to ease him down, he lost his grip. Mark fell on top of him, pulling the blanket that concealed the shotgun down with him, completely exposing the shotgun. It shifted to the edge of the shelf, but stopped just short of falling off. If the men had taken the time to look up, they would have seen the barrel hanging slightly over the edge. In the fall, neither man was hurt, but this led to a sequence of unkind words exchanged between them. Eager to hear what Mark had to reveal, Paul contained himself enough to display a spurious grin. He said, "My boy, no one is hurt, let's get back to the business at hand." Ignoring him, Mark turned his back furiously dusting off his hair and clothing, mumbling in disgust to himself for having to put up with Paul and his ostentatious ideas. He went to the kitchen sink and ran water over his head to clean himself. After he was satisfied that he was as clean as he was going to get, he rolled his eyes at Paul who was standing beside him, waiting on his report.

"There's no indication that anything has been hidden in the walls or stored up there."

"Are you sure?" asked Paul unconvinced.

"Hell no, I'm not sure! Go up there and see for yourself, cock-sucker! *Haennnnn!*"

Impulsively Paul swung at him, but in mid-air, he changed his mind. In anticipation of a strike, Mark ducked. "*Haennnnn!* Go ahead, try it, asshole!"

"Shut the fuck up! We don't have time for this shit!" Paul shouted turning his back on him to resume the search.

Completing their inspection of all the rooms except for one, they finally entered the backroom. They had developed a methodical pattern of tapping, then listening for any hollow sound. Periodically, Mark ceased searching to go to the door, making certain the coast was clear. While at the door, he heard Paul shouting excitedly, "I've found something! Come help me!" Mark looked upon Mrs. Caldwell and saw that she had managed to sit herself up. He made a quick assessment and decided she wasn't going anywhere.

With axes, the men tore up the floor to see what was underneath it. After several minutes of demolition, their excavation of the floorboards resulted in numerous piles of wood. The men stood on the floor's underlayment. Finding the secret door was a bonus because it made it easier for their descent. Paul's exhilaration was contagious. "We've hit pay dirt, my boy. I can feel it! I can feel it!" he reiterated. They walked down the stairs using a flashlight that they retrieved from their sack.

The men could not believe their eyes.

"Hot *diggety* dog!" shouted Paul with a wave of excitement.

"Yahoo! We're rich! Are we ever rich!" added Mark, fortifying his statement by dancing in a circle.

They walked around the dark cellar, touching several bars.

"What do you think these bars are worth?" asked Mark scratching his head.

Posing as an authoritative figure, Paul blurted out, "My estimation would be over a million dollars." Actually, he had no clue.

"Hey *looky* here, there's even crates to carry them in! Didn't we see crates like these in the middle of the backyard before we moved here?" he asked tilting his head in deep thought trying to recall.

It was too dark for them to see their faces with clarity, but they stood facing each other realizing the ineffaceable fact of conspiracy by the young couple.

"They've known the bullion was here all along," Paul cynically announced.

"They've been hogging the bullion for themselves," said Mark. "*Haennnn!* "They're *gonna* pay for this, especially that bitch," he added.

"They do deserve something, but we won't have time to serve them their 'just desserts,'" said Paul with the shrewdness of a conniving devil.

While the men loaded the bars of precious metal into the empty crates, Mrs. Caldwell tried to stand up against the couch. The searing pain from her head made it hard for her to pull herself up. She also fought against a nagging pain that was developing in her chest. Her only chance was to reach the telephone in the kitchen. On her belly, she inched her way toward the kitchen.

With only the aid of a single flashlight and the light that filtered down from the opening in the floor above, the men worked without noticing the lanterns hanging from the walls. After loading a few crates and testing their weight to make sure they could carry them, Paul told Mark, "Go and drive the car around the back. I'll continue to load the bars."

Mark ran up the stairs and once he reached the hall, he saw Mrs. Caldwell's body spread out across the floor. "Oh no you don't," he told her. He dragged her back to the living room and bound her hands and feet with rope. He left her battered body lying against a wall.

"Please don't do this, Mark," she implored.

"Now hush, Mrs. Caldwell, you don't want me to kick you, do you?"

The horrified woman didn't reply. Helplessly, she laid on the floor surrendering to a solitude of darkness.

34

Constantly on guard, when the men were in town, Louise made a habit of going home for lunch to keep a watchful eye on their house. The walk took her about seven minutes, therefore, she had enough time to eat something and get back to work. Clutching her handbag, Louise's brown penny loafers carried her swiftly through the streets.

Approaching her block, she noticed that both Mrs. Caldwell's and the men's vehicles were parked in front of the house. It was quite unusual to see Mrs. Caldwell's car this time of day. Since Deacon Reid's hospitalization, she spent her mid-days and afternoons visiting him. Louise decided to check on her to make certain she was alright before going in the house. Unlatching the gate, she ran up the stairs and rang Mrs. Caldwell's doorbell. Subsequently waiting for several moments without receiving a response, she knocked on the door and called out her name. Casually, Louise walked around to the backyard, anticipating to find Mrs. Caldwell stooped over working in her garden, but she was nowhere in sight. Glancing toward Mrs. Caldwell's house, she noticed the backdoor was open. Louise contemplated that Mrs. Caldwell must have reentered the house and she missed her while she walked around to the back.

"Mrs. Caldwell, are you in there?" Louise shouted at the backdoor. Not waiting for an answer, automatically she entered the house. On the kitchen table, Louise wistfully ran her fingers over Mrs. Caldwell's purse, a half gallon of milk, which needed storing in the refrigerator, along with paper bags containing meat and other items.

Something was amiss. Louise recalled that Mrs. Caldwell had not been feeling well and assumed she was somewhere in the house. Searching each room, Louise called out to her, fearing that she had a heart attack or stroke. Not finding her rattled her nerves. Short of panicking, she considered, *Perhaps, Mrs. Caldwell is visiting a neighbor and forgot to put her things away.* No, her intuition told her something was definitely wrong. As heinous thoughts plagued her, she wondered where the men were. Were they upstairs because if they were, it was awfully quiet up there? Did they know where she was, or even worse had they done something to harm her? *Don't be foolish,* she conjured, *Mrs. Caldwell is probably emptying the garbage.* Louise left out of the backdoor, in search of her.

A few feet away from her own house, Louise discovered the door was open. Being the last one to leave in the morning, she knew she had not left it open. Surely, if there was some kind of dilemma and Mrs. Caldwell needed to gain entry to their place, she would have contacted Louise at the store. A red flag went up and without bothering to enter, she eased backward and hastily retreated for Mrs. Caldwell's backdoor.

)0(

Exiting the coach house to get the car, Mark noticed Louise rushing away from her house. In a swift pursuit, he ran up behind her and tackled her down to the ground. Mark was unprepared for the vicious counterattack Louise issued. His earlier assessment of her was that she was all talk, therefore, he had not taken her seriously. While tussling on the ground, Louise's voice raised to shrieking screams. She struck out at him scratching his face, hands, and arms perniciously. To shut her up, quickly, he stuffed her mouth with the filthy handkerchief he used to clean himself with after scrounging around in the attic crawl space. She gagged as she tried to expunge it from her mouth. Overpowering Louise, he wrapped his hand around her hair and pulled her up to a standing position. After several attempts of her falling to the ground in defiance, he succeeded in twisting her arm behind her back. Louise was seething. Her tormented facial expression would have warded off most demons, but not the fool that held her captive. The short walk to her house was not a cooperative one, because she resisted him on every step. She stumped on his feet, forcing him to tighten his rein on her arm, consequently, making her docile in compliance. Her hope was that someone might have heard or seen her.

Upon entering the house, Mark started to take her to the living room to bind her in a chair until a muttered sound escaped from Mrs. Caldwell on the floor. Louise tried to walk over to her but Mark's steadfast hold of her was unrelenting. She saw Mrs. Caldwell's feet and legs then tried harder to free herself, succeeding in spitting the handkerchief from her mouth.

"You miserable cockroach! What have you done to Mrs. Caldwell? Let me go to her and help her!" she insisted.

"Shut up, bitch!" shouted Mark, releasing his hand from her arm and slapping her across the back of her head with his hand.

The force from the blow rendered her into submission. The air was thick from the abhorrence Louise harbored toward him, noticeable by her insolent stance.

Strategically altering her demeanor, Louise beseeched him to let her tend to Mrs. Caldwell. Inflexibly ignoring her, he cloistered and shoved Louise into her bedroom. "You high and mighty nigger, I'm *gonna* show you whose the boss around here." Spinning her around he ripped her blue blouse, causing buttons to fly off into the air. He pushed Louise on the bed and she tried to roll off of it. He jumped on top of her fondling and kissing her. Desperately, she needed to figure out a way to escape from him. When he tackled her in the yard, she dropped her purse, which housed the knife Dennis had given her for protection. Now, she wished she had kept it in her pocket. Lying on top of her, Mark stretched her arms out to the sides, pinning her down. Shifting her face from side to side, she frantically tried to avoid his slobbery kisses. When his appalling slippery tongue entered her mouth, ferociously she bit down on it. He let out a howl, immediately releasing Louise affording her the opportunity to shove her elbow into his face. Taking only a few seconds to recoup, he hit her in the eye with his fist. "Bitch! Come on, let's play. *Haennnnn!* I'm beginning to enjoy this!" He slapped her repeatedly across her face and chest, forcing her to holler and cowl away from him. Mark started to knock her in the abdomen with his knee, but she flinched and curled up, trying to protect her mid-section.

"Please don't hurt me, I'm expecting a baby!" she begged.

He said, "I ought to knock that baby out of your stomach! One more move like that, and you'll find my fist in your gut! Do you understand me?"

Louise nodded.

"Alrighty then, let's see some cooperation around here. You know what I want! *Haennnnn!*"

"So that country nigger of yours, done knocked you up! What did he do that for? That's all we need is another *fuckin'* nigger child in this world. I've never screwed a pregnant bitch before, let's see if there's a difference," he mocked with malevolence.

She wanted to inform him that he was the degenerate who did not belong on this earth. Through her civility, she forced herself to keep her cool by not responding to his sickening remarks.

Positioning himself back on top of her, his grotesque tongue played with her lips. Cringing, Louise tightly closed her eyes and turned her head trying to escape from him. Mark rewarded her with an atrocious bite on the tip of her nose. She cried out in pain. "I warned you, bitch, you better cooperate! This is what you get for being an uppity nigger, trying to hide the bullion from us!"

Saddened that Dennis was not there to save her, she stared at Mark with both scorn and disappointment. She and Dennis failed in protecting the bullion and saving it for themselves. *Oh Dennis, I wish you were here to help me.* Tears of frustration trickled down the sides of her face.

As his captive, she was forced to listen in disgust to his idiotic boasting about how clever he was, and what he was going to do with her. Endlessly, he chattered while she fleetingly watched him remove his clothing from the waist down. Louise bucked when he eased onto the bed with a knife, which he had produced from his pants pocket. Waving it in the air, he brought the knife down and made a cutting gesture across her belly. Cursing as she knocked the knife away from him, he slapped her across her face. In an attempt to get away from him, she leaped from the bed and ran out of the room. He ran after her, flying through the air and tackling her down. Louise fought as if for her life, while they wrestled on the floor. Her struggle to free herself from him was for the dual purpose of saving herself and her unborn child. Kicking and scratching at him did not deter him. Jubilantly, Mark fought her, her actions brought on his excitement, which was displayed by his erection. He toyed with her as if she was a mouse, by allowing her to put distance between them, then pouncing upon her until she tired. Pleased with himself for diminishing her strength to fight, he carried her into the bedroom.

Retrieving his knife off the floor, he expertly used it to cut a couple of strips from the sheet in order to tie her hands to each side of the headboard. As he performed this task, she could tell he had done this dirty deed several times before. Teasing her with the knife, he ran it across her breast before placing it in the crevice between her breasts cutting away her bra. He groped her breast with his hands, then raised her skirt and hastily cut away her underwear. The trepidation of being slashed by his knife made Louise quiver.

Proudly, the fool stood over her. He bragged, "*Haennnnn!* You're *gonna* get Willy here. Yeah he's ready, *willin'* and able. *Haennnnn!*" grasping and shaking himself at her. "I've been dreaming about this day," he said with enthusiasm, discarding the knife by throwing it on top of his clothes. Since their initial meeting, his insatiable desire for her had grown. He had not allowed himself complete sexual satisfaction from anyone else and the anticipation of violating Louise was overwhelming. "Who knows? You might even enjoy it. *Haennnnn!*" As his demeanor changed to a more sinister one, he added, "You and that country nigger of yours have been holding out on us. You planned on keeping the bullion for yourselves. This is what you deserve, bitch!" He spoke with malevolent confidence. Louise laid in terror, mentally preparing herself to endure his injustices upon her.

35

Paul assiduously stacked and placed the bullion in crates. Under most circumstances, he preferred not to exert himself, but in this instance, it was only a minuscule bother. He pushed a wooden laden crate toward the stairs with the aid of his foot. Paul was so absorbed in his chore that he had lost track of time, until he heard unwarranted shouting and thumps filtering down from the floor above. Initially, he contemplated that Mrs. Caldwell had come to, and Mark had to "resituate" her, but the old woman could not have been that much trouble. When the commotion did not cease, he took the stairs two at a time to investigate.

Mark was kneeling over Louise whose face was bruised and swollen. He was just about to place himself between her legs. "What the fuck do you think you're doing?" shouted Paul. "I don't have time for you to play games." Grappling the back of Mark's shirt, he swung him off the bed. Mark cursed sadistically at him. "Get your goddamn clothes back on and go get the car like I told you to," roared Paul. His veins extended across his forehead and more popped out on the sides of his neck.

"But I couldn't, she came home and discovered us. I had to do something to shut her up!" Mark proclaimed in frustration.

"So screwing her is going to make her shut up? You're *fuckin'* unbelievable! Get the hell out of here! Get out of here now before I kill you! When we finish this job I swear, I'm *gonna* dump your ass!"

Obediently, Mark did as he was told. Shaking his head in disgust, Paul was not completely surprised by Mark's behavior because it was characteristic of the kind of havoc he often caused. Under the circumstances, he thought Mark could have used better judgment. Paul gave Louise the once over, decided that in her condition she was not a threat, and returned to the cellar.

)0(

The crates were too large to fit into their car so one by one they placed the bars of precious metal into the trunk, cautiously watching to make sure no one saw them. Paul chortled that if they were seen, no one would believe that the bars were real anyway. While the men loaded the vehicle, Louise struggled to free herself. Her adrenaline did not allow her to feel the pain from the bruises she acquired from battling with her antagonist. Casting aside her own troubles, she worried about Mrs. Caldwell. Was she going to be alright? She could hear the men struggling with a crate coming from the backroom and knocking it against a wall as they walked through the house. Vulnerably, she laid ensnared, wondering how she could stop them.

The men passed by her bedroom without giving her any thought. She kept her eyes peeled to the door, remaining motionless. Louise did not have time to dwell on the fact that she was partially clothed, and feeling humiliated was a minute issue. Luckily, she escaped violation from the weasel. She had Paul to thank for that, construing he possessed some scruples after all. Fraught to free herself, Louise finally loosened the binding on one of her wrists enough to slip a hand free. Turning on her side and scooting up toward the side of the headboard, she used her teeth and free hand to untie the sheet. She picked up the receiver to the telephone and started to dial for help, but one of the men was reentering the house. Swiftly, she eased back on the bed and rearranged her clothing. She did not have enough time to reposition the strips from the sheet around her hands, so she raised her arms placing her hands under the sheet. Paul looked down on her as he snatched the telephone from the wall, throwing it onto the kitchen floor. When he passed the room on the way out, he noticed the close proximity of the telephone, which sat on the nightstand, next to the bed. He also took time to cut the wire to the telephone in the kitchen. Taking a break from his work, he stood over Louise, lit a cigarette, and admired her legs. Distress reeked across her face.

"Don't worry, Louise, I won't touch you now, but I don't want you to call the police for a couple of hours after Mark and I leave. We need time to disappear. If the police come after us and catch us, I'll personally come back here and kill you. Do you understand?" he asked with a manifestation that was menacing.

"But Mrs. Caldwell needs help!"

"That's tough! Do what you can for her, but don't call the police!"

Once Paul finished his cigarette, he threw the butt on the floor and rejoined Mark.

The shotgun in the kitchen pantry was Louise's only hope of redemption, if they had not discovered it already. Rising from the bed, as she stood her wrinkled skirt fell into place. Her torn blouse flew open as she ran to the window and warily pulled back the curtain. Louise observed the men unloading the contents of a crate into their car. The work was tedious. They were constantly lifting and placing bars neatly in the vehicle so they would have plenty of room for all of them. Taking this opportunity to check on Mrs. Caldwell, she rushed to the living room. The poor elderly woman was lying quietly on the floor. The sight of blood on the side of her head traumatized Louise. She blamed herself, for not speaking up and convincing everyone about her acuity regarding the men. Their behavior was precisely what she expected from them. Squatting beside her landlord, Louise whispered, "I'm here, Mrs. Caldwell. Hold on, please, I'll try to get you some help." The sound of her own voice was foreign to her because it was cracked from screaming and fighting with Mark. Whether the ailing woman was cognizant of her presence, she could not tell. Louise heard the back gate squeak as the men reentered the yard. Returning to the bed she elevated her skirt enough so that only her legs showed, then wrapped the strips from the sheet around her wrists, repositioning herself the way she thought the men had left her.

)0(

After she was sure that Mark and Paul were down in the secret cellar, she treaded softly to the kitchen pantry. Louise became flustered when she saw the blanket on the floor, fearing that the men had discovered the shotgun. In the likelihood that it was on the shelf, she looked up high and saw the shotgun. *It is still here,* she smiled. Before she could grasp it, she heard the men struggling up the stairs with another load. Foregoing the attempt to get the shotgun, she ran back to the bed. Walking backward with his load, Mark looked in on her as he passed the room with a smirk on his face. Holding onto the strips that remained around the side of the headboard, she acted as if she was genuinely trying to free herself. When Paul saw that Mark was distracted, he shoved his end of the crate into Mark causing him to stagger and curse. "That wasn't necessary!" Mark snapped back at him.

When the coast was clear, Louise rushed to the kitchen pantry. On her tiptoes, she used her fingertips to pull the shotgun down. She ran back to the bedroom and hid it underneath the bed. Despising the unsubtle threat Paul issued to her, she was not about to allow a convict to subject her to some form of repression. After the mental torment and sacrifices she experienced in leaving her home in Avinger, Texas, and finally reaching a point of acceptance of her new life and the happiness it offered, it would be a cold day in hell before she let him be a disruption. Nor was she going to allow the convicts to get away with harming Mrs. Caldwell, or her narrow escape from being raped, or the beating she received from Mark. Her psyche boiled and the only resolution was to inhibit the men from initiating anymore pandemonium. Impatiently, Louise waited until she heard the men's descent below.

Seizing the shotgun, she tipped placidly to the backroom attempting not to make any noise. The floorboards of the old building creaked. Hesitating on every few steps, Louise moved toward the backroom, expecting to be discovered at any moment. She heard the men talking and organizing themselves for the upward ascent.

Mark mounted the stairs backwards, struggling to hold his end of the voluminous load. As he reached the second stair from the top landing, his back touched the cold steel of the open end of the shotgun. "Don't take anymore steps or I'll be forced to shoot you," Louise demanded boldly. This startled Mark because it was unbelievable that she held a gun up against his back. Shifting his body around to see what was touching him, he lost his footing. Slackening his grip on the crate, he watched it slip from his fingers, making Paul the sole recipient of the weighed crate. Paul plummeted backward down the stairs under the full force of the crate, and the bullion scattered everywhere.

Mark laughed nervously, "*Haennnnn!* You really don't want to shoot me now, do you?"

"Try me!" exclaimed Louise, the only response she offered.

Raising his hands in the air, he swung around quickly, challenging her by reaching for the shotgun. In an instant, he succeeded in snatching it from her and knocking her to the floor. A shot went off and Louise rolled out the way to avoid it. The piercing sound of the gunshot was not as audible as the lurid noise from the bullion tumbling down the stairs and landing on the floor of the cellar. Mark stood startled that he had not gotten shot. He said, "Bitch, wait 'til I get my hands on you!" Like a stubborn mule, Louise got on all fours and kicked her legs out at Mark as hard as she could. Consequently, he fell backwards, hitting his head on the floor before falling down the stairs.

The shotgun flew out of his hands and landed on the floor of the cellar. Without hesitation, Louise tackled the stairs to search for it. The moment she reached the bottom stair, Mark grabbed her leg making her fall on top of him. He scowled in pain from the bruises he sustained from the fall. With outstretched hands, they scrambled around on the floor in semi darkness searching for the lost shotgun. Mark tried to stand, but hadn't realized that he had broken his right leg in the fall. He tried pulling Louise toward him and succeeded in knocking her against a wooden crate. Louise raked her hands over the bullion and found the shotgun. The lighting was poor but enough for Mark to see that Louise had the shotgun in her hands. He threw a gold bar in her direction. Dodging it, she cocked the shotgun and released the trigger. A bullet entered into Mark's chest.

He let out a terrible wail. "Bitch, you shot me! I hope you die in hell." He fell on his back and laid frozen in place.

She walked over and nudged Mark with the end of the shotgun, making certain that he was no longer a threat to her. "It shouldn't have come to this, you freak!" Louise proclaimed.

In his weakened condition, Mark uttered a low moan. She left him on his back to listen to the blood as it gurgled from his chest. Before tackling the stairs, Louise picked up the flashlight, and walked over to examine Paul. He remained motionless. She remounted the stairs and went to check on Mrs. Caldwell.

Louise untied the rope from Mrs. Caldwell's hands and feet. The condition of the older woman was grave. "I'm here, Mrs. Caldwell, please wake up."

Mrs. Caldwell opened her eyes. "Mark did this to me and…," she said barely able to speak.

"Hush now, Mrs. Caldwell save your strength," said Louise, rubbing her hands and feet to get some circulation back in them. "I've got to go to your house to use the telephone to call the police and get you an ambulance. I'll be right back."

The older woman nodded. She grabbed Louise's hand to signal that she was grateful. "Hurry back," said Mrs. Caldwell faintly.

)0(

By the time the police and ambulance arrived, Louise had changed into something decent. Immediately, Mrs. Caldwell was whisked away in the ambulance.

"What happened here?" inquired one of the officers.

Louise explained in detail what she discovered when she arrived home early from work. The police officers called in for assistance and two detectives arrived. The officers converged on the cellar and took pictures before bringing Mark up in a stretcher. He was pronounced dead on the spot.

"Mrs. Clark, I thought you said there were two men downstairs. We only found one," said Detective Martinelli, as they watched Mark's body being removed from the house.

"There were two men down there. Mark and Paul, but Paul's his real name is Kevin Tatum."

"Ma'am, you want to show me."

Louise returned to the cellar and showed them where she had left both men lying on the floor. Now the room was brightly lit because all the lanterns were on. "Paul was lying there," Louise, pointed to the spot with her finger. "See there is a bloodstain in the dirt."

"Take a sample of this blood for me, Joe," said the detective to the lab technician.

Befuddled, Louise look around the cellar to see if Paul was hiding somewhere. She couldn't understand how Paul managed to escape. He appeared unconscious and didn't display any signs of life while she struggled with Mark. Her actual assessment was that he was dead. She ran back upstairs to her living room and looked out of the window. "There was a car, a black Ford sedan, out there. Didn't you see it when you arrived?"

"No, ma'am," was the detective's response.

Louise rattled off everything she could remember about Paul. His demeanor, how he dressed and spoke.

"What was the license plate number to the car?" asked Detective Saunders.

"I don't know. I don't recall ever paying it much attention. The men lived upstairs on the second floor."

The detectives sent a couple of men to search on the second floor of Mrs. Caldwell's building. They returned and announced, "Mrs. Clark, the apartment upstairs is mostly empty except for furniture and a few of their personal belongings."

In shock, Louise's response was, "This is unbelievable."

"Mrs. Clark, how do you know that Kevin Tatum was using an alias?" asked Detective Martinelli.

"Uh, I overheard Mark say his name when he thought no one was listening." she said.

"When was that?"

"I was working in my garden and the men were coming through the yard to empty the garbage."

"What actually did they say? Do you recall?"

"Uh, that nobody knows your real name is Kevin Tatum. Uh, that's when I began to have some suspicions that the men were up to something."

"Why was that?" asked Detective Martinelli.

Louise knew she had to be careful not implicate herself, so she repeated what Mrs. Blunt told her. "I say one of them looking around the house at doors and the windows."

"He was probably searching for the bullion," said Detective Saunders.

"Maybe so," said Louise feeling confident that she had not incriminated herself.

36

At the construction site, a worker wearing a hard hat exited the crane elevator by jumping off of it onto one of the upper floors in search of Dennis. "Dennis Clark! Is Dennis Clark up here?" he asked having to shout above the sound of welding.

One of the crew members addressed him by saying, "If you're looking for Dennis Clark he's over there!" pointing to a couple of men who were unfastening cables from the end of a steel beam.

"Hello! Are either of you Dennis Clark?" the guy asked shouting over the noise.

"Yeah, I'm Clark!" announced Dennis glancing up. "Why? What do you want?"

"The boss said you got a call from your wife! Go see him for more information!"

"Is there anything wrong?"

"Hey, I'm just the messenger, man! Go see Mr. Stern in his office!"

"Thanks!" replied Dennis.

)0(

Dennis did not have a sense of what to expect on his way home. His boss repeated Louise's exact words, "Come home, there's been an emergency." Things had gone well for them, probably too well, because they were fortunate for being gainfully employed, living in a nice little house, and were expecting a child. He vowed no matter what the problem was that they would work through it. The worse thing he could imagine was that Louise aborted their baby, and if that was the case, he would be sorrowful and would give her all the support he could. Perhaps something had happened to Mrs. Caldwell, but she should have been at the hospital visiting Deacon Reid.

His inquisitive turmoil served as a distraction. He was driving too close to the center lane when a bus made a wide turn onto the same street. To avoid a collision, Dennis swerved in the opposite direction just in time. Pedestrians watched as he ended up on the curb next to a lamppost, luckily, without hitting anyone or doing any damage to his truck. Taking a few moments to regain his composure, he sat in the truck next to the curb resting his head on the steering wheel before proceeding.

Approaching Iroquois Street, he noticed that the police had set up road blocks on the street and alley. It appeared to be in close proximity of his house. Finding available parking around the corner, he jogged to the mouth of the alley.

"Can't go through the alley," announced the police officer sitting in the parked car blocking access to the alley. Dennis observed people huddling in their yards and standing around the area that was roped off. Parked police vehicles and ambulances were near his back gate.

"I live there," he said with urgency, pointing to where the vehicles sat and trying not to panic. "My wife called my job and left word for me to come home." After showing his identification, the officer allowed him to pass.

A suffocating tightness dwelled in his chest as he tried to envision what could possibly be wrong that would attract all this attention. Why was Louise home early from work? Did she go to work? There was no indication before he left home that she was ill. She must have been feeling fairly decent, since she personally called his job. Sniffing the air, he tried to ascertain if there had been a fire, but there was no trace of smoke. His unanswered questions made his intestines turn into knots, cramping his stomach. He jogged the short distance to his back gate. Once he reached the ambulance, he peeked inside and saw a white sheet covering someone. Baffled, with wrinkled lines forming across his brow, he asked, "What happened?" questioning the officer standing at the gate. The officer directed him to continue to the house.

What tragedy had befallen upon his house? Picking up his pace, he practically ran to his door where he met several officers who were hauling out crates of the bullion.

"What has happened?" he repeated. "Is my wife alright?" Thwarted with more fear now that he knew the bullion was involved.

"She'll be okay, go inside, they are expecting you," said one of the men.

After entering his house, a plain clothed officer walked over to him. He said, "Hello. Are you Mr. Clark?"

"Yes, I am," he replied, nervously fumbling with his keys.

The officer extended his hand by pumping it. He announced, "Hello sir, I'm Detective Saunders and my partner over there is Detective Martinelli." He motioned to the detective sitting at the kitchen table with Louise. Saunders stood over six feet tall with broad shoulders blocking Dennis' view of Louise.

"Congratulations for having such a brave lady for your wife."

"Thanks," drawled out Dennis puzzled by what the man meant. At the kitchen table, plenty of activity surrounded Louise. People were there from the crime lab, a photographer was loading new film in his camera at one end of the kitchen table, and police officers were walking all through the house. Another detective was questioning Louise and taking notes.

Dennis was unprepared for the vicarious sight in front of him. Uncannily, Louise's face was puffy and badly bruised. A bandage was positioned across her nose, and her right eye was blackened and partially closed. Who could have done such an unforgiving thing to his beautiful wife? "Lou, what happened?" he asked as his lower lip quivered.

Louise rushed up from the table into his arms.

"Are you alright?" he asked. "What happened? Who did this to you, Lou?" he asked with grave concern, examining her by lightly touching her swollen face and patting down her disheveled hair.

"Yes, honey, I'm fine. I'm so glad you're home."

"Who's in the ambulance?" he inquired.

Through sobs of tears and gargled speech, she tried to explain. The only thing Dennis was able to decipher was that Mark attacked her and something about Mrs. Caldwell lying hurt.

"Did he hurt you?" he interrupted her.

"Only a little."

"What do you mean?" he said sternly, his whole body was upright and rigid.

"He only beat me up and nothing more," was her reply.

"And nothing more?" he repeated glowering with vengeance. "Where is the bastard? I want to see him!" he demanded.

The officers stood at attention prepared to subdue him.

Using the back of her hand to wipe away her tears, Louise composed herself enough to say, "Those men, Mark and Paul, were in search of buried treasure, the gold and silver bars that the police are taking out of our house." She gestured with her head to the police officers who were making several trips with hand dollies to remove the bullion. "Dennis, they somehow figured out that the bullion was hidden in a secret cellar underneath our house, apparently for several years. I told the officers that we didn't know anything about the treasure, and that we've only lived here for a short time," she continued. Carefully guarding her speech, she focused in on Dennis' eyes, fervently hoping that she was persuasive in her ambiguous statement.

Detective Martinelli took over from there, explaining in detail what happened according to their investigation and the explanation they received from Louise.

"Your wife here is responsible for saving some of the secret treasure from the hands of the two criminals that were out on parole. You were sitting on top of a gold mine and didn't know it," he chuckled.

"Gold mine, treasure, huh?" repeated Dennis nodding his head to Louise, acknowledging that he completely understood her.

"Yeah, the bars have Spanish inscriptions on them and we will have someone investigate its origin," said Detective Martinelli. "Mrs. Clark shot and killed Mark Parker in self defense. Paul Nielsen alias Kevin Tatum fell down the stairs backwards but somehow was able to get away. We have a warrant out for his arrest and will probably catch him in no time," continued the detective.

Dennis' expression was one of undeniable disbelief because Louise had undergone such an ordeal. He scoped her body before asking her numerous questions.

"Weren't you afraid? What made you leave work to come home and…Lou, are you sure you're alright?" he finally said.

"Yes, especially now that you're home," she replied, reaching for his hand and smiling.

"They also beat up Mrs. Caldwell and she's in the hospital."

"How is she doing?"

"I don't know," said Louise earnestly, looking toward the detectives for an answer.

"A call came in over the radio," interrupted Detective Saunders. "One of the officers who was leaving your house as you came in sir, reported to me that the old lady, uh excuse me, your landlord, Mrs. Caldwell, experienced a massive heart attack. She did not survive. I'm sorry." The detective looked down at his writing pad to reference Mrs. Caldwell's name, when he reported the terrible news.

"Oh, no, no, no…," sobbed Louise. "How could they have done this to her? Mrs. Caldwell didn't deserve this! She couldn't have caused them any trouble. They didn't have to harm her! Oh Dennis! She is…she was like a mother to me!"

Dennis and Louise clung to each other, seeking solace from the beleaguered news. Losing equanimity, their tears flowed. Both detectives excused themselves from the kitchen in order to give the young couple some privacy.

After some time had passed, the detectives returned and informed them that a wallet belonging to Rufus Reid was found underneath the bed in the back bedroom. Louise gave Dennis a self righteous stare as Dennis explained to the officer who Deacon Reid was, and what had happened to him. The police officers were pleased with themselves for having solved another case.

Detective Martinelli informed the Clarks that it was necessary to advise Mrs. Caldwell's next of kin regarding her death. Louise was escorted through the backdoor of Mrs. Caldwell's house and she found the information they needed. She asked permission to be the one to tell Mrs. Caldwell's children about their mother.

37

Paul presumed he was safe for the time being. Weighing his options, if he didn't show up for work, a call would be made to his parole officer and someone would be in search of him. No one knew his real name, therefore, he could probably continue working for the railroad company. The two things that were imminently necessary were getting rid of his car and the bullion. He had an amiable association with a pawn shop broker who knew a welder, who could melt the bullion down for a fee.

Although the welder wasn't far away, Paul couldn't take the chance of driving around in his current vehicle. With sufficient money to get a room or a small apartment somewhere, he opted to stay at Betty's, his casual friend. He met her a year ago in the bar where she worked in the evenings. Betty allowed him to park his car and store his belonging in her garage. After she left for work, Paul removed the bullion from his trunk, stacked it in a corner of the garage, and covered it with burlap bags and other miscellaneous junk.

At the pawn shop, he showed the broker a couple of pieces of his bullion.

"Where did you get this? he asked.

"Maybe, its best that you don't know. How much do you think I can get for it after it's melted down?"

"If you have as much as you say you do, probably a little less than a $500 Gs," he answered

"That's all!"

"Yeah man, this stuff is hot and the alloy can probably be linked to its source."

"Really. "Well, you can have ten percent of whatever I get for it."

"No, that's not good enough, I want forty percent. I'm making this happen for you and I'm paying for the melt down."

"I'm not giving you that much. You haven't earned it. You can have twenty-five percent."

"Hell, no! I want thirty-five and nothing less," the broker demanded.

"You're such a bastard! This is highway robbery!"

"Take it or leave it!"

"Okay, thirty-five percent," Paul said with reluctance.

They shook on it.

Paul felt the pawn broker was greedy as hell and everything he came upon was linked to a price tag. *But, wasn't he in the business of making money,* he resolved.

The next day the broker told Paul that the bullion was too hot and that there was a state alert out for it. It would have to be put on ice for the time being. Blatantly disappointed, Paul redirected his focus on the prospect of what he would acquire when the timing was right.

)0(

When Paul reported to work, he went in the office to get his assignment. They asked about Mark and he told them that he hadn't seen him. Subsequently finishing a two week run on the rail line, Paul went to the office to pick up his paycheck and new schedule. While he was waiting, he went over to an empty telephone booth to call Betty.

"Betty, my dear, I'm in off the road, how about spending a night on the town with me?" asked Paul feeling rather good about himself.

Cheerfully she replied, "Darlin', I've got to work at the tavern tonight. Why don't you join me at the bar for drinks?"

"That'll work, I'm on my way to your…"

"Excuse me, are you Kevin Tatum alias Paul Nielsen?" asked Detective Martinelli pushing the door in to open the telephone booth. "You're under arrest for the death of Florence Caldwell, robbery, and assault. Where is the bullion?"

Paul uttered in disbelief, "Uh huh." His tonsils flared in anger as he tried to buck out of the door but Martinelli and Saunders' huge bulkiness blocked his path. Viciously, Paul fought the men off, refusing to surrender easily. This was his biggest scheme ever and captivity would prohibit him from wreaking its benefit. He was pissed off. This debacle was almost beyond his comprehension. Was his destiny always to be a failure?

"Who were you talking to on the phone?" asked Martinelli. Paul refused to answer. Martinelli picked up the phone. "Hello, who is this?" There was a click before the phone went dead.

"Give him his rights," he told Saunders after they subdued Paul by handcuffing him.

"You have the right to remain silent…," started the detective.

Defeat wasn't something that Paul wanted to accept. Assuming Mark was dead, even in his death, he couldn't escape him. Faulting Mark for being a blabbermouth and originally mentioning that they worked for the railroad company, then Paul blamed himself for partnering up with him and not foreseeing his immediate capture. He should have left town, but couldn't chance being caught with the bullion. Vehemently, he cursed at the detectives. "Don't touch me!" he declared. Ignoring him, they handcuffed him.

Paul walked out of the office with his head up high. The rail employees talked about him as he passed. Fuck you! Fuck all of you!" he spat at them contemptuously.

)0(

So sure of themselves, Paul and Mark packed their belongings and deposited them at the Betty's house the day before they broke into Dennis and Louise's house. "We're going out of town for a while and I must give up my apartment," he told her. He shoved seventy-five dollars in her hand to pacify her. He was out the door before she could ask him any questions.

When Paul fell down the stairs to the cellar, he landed in the dirt. His back hurt from the fall, and his head and chest were battered by some of the bullion. Even though there was a gash in his head, the pain wasn't unbearable. Once he realized Louise had a shotgun, he played possum contemplating he would venture out when it was safe. After all, it wasn't his forte to be a violent man, that was the reason he kept Mark around. He wasn't a pushover by any means, his preference was reasoning over violence.

While Louise tended to Mrs. Caldwell, he eased up the stairs. When she left to use the old lady's telephone, he snuck out to his car but realized he didn't have the keys. Returning to the house he eased passed the living room unnoticeable by Mrs. Caldwell.

Without the aid of the flashlight, he fumbled around in the darken cellar. The quieting stillness of the room was uncanny. Stumbling over some bars, then Mark's leg, he bent over confronted with the grotesque task of padding down a dead man's body. Feeling for the keys, he struggled to get his hand inside Mark's pants pocket. They were lying close to his inner thigh. *Ohhhhhh*," moaned Mark reaching and grabbing Paul's hand. In horror, Paul released a throaty howl and snatched his hand away because he undoubtedly thought his cohort was dead. Hovering over him Paul said, "Sorry my boy, I can't help you," and then he ran up the stairs with the keys.

When he passed the kitchen, he saw Louise exiting Mrs. Caldwell's backdoor. He couldn't take the chance of being seen. On the kitchen table in clear view sat the shotgun. He debated, *What can I accomplish by using it? If I leave out the door to the coach house Louise will see me.* He was positive Mrs. Caldwell was unconscious because he didn't hear any movement from her. He opted to exit from the broken window in the living room, the same way Mark originally entered the house.

Rushing to the window his eyes interlocked with Mrs. Caldwell who was lying on the floor. She paled at the sight of him causing crusting pangs of pressure to develop in her chest. Paul bounced out the window and hopped over the fence. *I'm too old for this shit,* he panted. In the alley, he squatted on his knees between the car and the fence. Once Louise entered the coach house, he got in his car and drove off.

)0(

Paul spent the next six years in a familiar confining place. His sentence was lessened since Louise testified that Mrs. Caldwell said that Mark was the one that hurt her. Throughout his trial, Paul maintained a loathsome smirk because he had orchestrated it all. His refusal to divulge the location of the bullion added a couple of years to his time. Even after his sentencing, he seemed to be triumphantly gloating with his private dreams of opulence. *Fuck all of them. I'll be a rich man, something they'll never achieve. A nice way to spend my golden years.* He chuckled.

)0(

Subsequent to settling back in the prison system, Paul sent word to Betty at the tavern through an inmate for her to take care of his things. Her returned message guaranteed him that she would take good care of everything. They couldn't exchange letters because the authorities monitored all correspondence. The day of his release from prison, Paul was older, and perhaps a little more worn. He saw himself as a changed man, desiring a new life. Tired of pulling scams on people, now he wouldn't have to. His dream to own a restaurant had dwindled. A simpler life is what he sought. Freedom was his priority, an occasional *magnifique* meal, and to sleep on brisk, clean sheets.

A room was waiting for him at the YMCA, and that would do for a start. Arrangements were made for him to work as a janitor at a fishery. His intention to do this was only until he finished his parole. He longed for a place of his own somewhere near the ocean. Perhaps he'd buy himself a Cadillac and take it out on the road whenever he felt the urge.

Before checking into the Y, he took a bus to Betty's house. There were children playing in her front yard. With their eyes, they followed him as he walked.

"May I help you," asked a young woman instantly appearing at the door.

"Hello, miss, I'm looking for Betty. Is she around?"

Gawking at him blankly, she replied, "There is no Betty here. Maybe you have the wrong address."

"No, this is where she lives," he insisted.

"I'm sorry sir, but my family and I have been living here for three years now. Before we moved in, there was an elderly couple living here. Perhaps, my next door neighbor can help you. Children, time to come in," she called out.

Beads of sweat formed upon his face unrelated to the hot, California sun. The lightweight clothing that Paul wore didn't give him much relief as anxiety grew within him. He fanned himself as he went from door to door of a few of the neighboring houses, but no one could help him locate Betty. A friendly neighbor offered him a glass of water to quench what she thought was thirst. But Paul's thirst could not be quenched by water only his precious bars of gold and silver bullion could do the job.

Too early for the tavern to be open, he checked into the Y. To pass time he walked around his new neighborhood taking in what it had to offer. By late afternoon, he entered Betty's tavern, but it didn't have any resemblance to the way it looked before. It was modernistic with decorative walls and fancy chrome chairs. The staff wore uniforms and when he inquired about Betty none of them knew her. Paul was advised that the owner might be able to help him but he wasn't due in until later. To settle his underlying panic Paul found a nearby restaurant and got a bite to eat. Once he returned to the tavern, he was directed to a guy in the back.

"Hey, Tom how in the hell are you?" asked Paul to the man's back.

"My name is Don, what can I do for you, Bud?"

"Uh, I...I'm looking for Tom the other owner. Doesn't he still own this place?

"Sorry, Bud, he retired, I bought this place from him a few years ago. Is there anything I can do for you?"

"Do you know Betty Sutton? Paul described the way she looked the last time he saw her.

"I'm sorry, Bud, but I don't know her."

)0(

For years, Paul scoured the city for Betty, but she was no where to be found. Paul's dreams were crushed. The thought of losing his precious treasure was maddening. He developed a behavioral twitch, whereas, he jerked his head as if clearing his thoughts. Ironically, he was doomed to spend his time working as a janitor at the smelly fishery that left him with a daily stench. Good hygiene and clean fingernails became less important. The once cunning and conniving conman could be seen mumbling to himself while mopping a floor.

)0(

A madam sat on the balcony of her newly built hotel overlooking the street below. She cooled herself from the day's heat, by fanning with a scone-shaped fan that advertised Madam Bee's Haven of Luxury. She reflected over her new life of wealth. Like raindrops, things seemed to have fallen into her lap. Several months after Paul's arrest the pawn broker collected the bullion from her garage paying her a generous amount. Surreptitiously, she packed her belongings and took the Pacific Atlantic train straight to New Orleans, the home of her great-grandfather.

38

The experience Louise had undergone was devastating, and trying to find peace of mind was difficult after losing Mrs. Caldwell and having taken Mark's life. She tried to convince herself that killing Mark was no different than ridding herself of a fly that was a nuisance, but it was not that simple. He was entitled to live his roguish life, the same as she was entitled to live hers, even though he was responsible for Mrs. Caldwell's death. Rehashing the events at Paul's trial didn't make things any easier, but knowing that Paul was to be held accountably for his and Mark's actions bought her some satisfaction.

From the love she shared with her husband, coupled with the comfort she received from her family and friends, she found a place of tranquility. Giving birth to her daughter was appeasing. It allowed her to find closure to a bad chapter in her life. Louise and Dennis named their daughter Flora after their landlord. Their baby represented everything that was innocent and pure. The new responsibilities of caring for Flora brought emanated joy and happiness to the young Clark's household.

)0(

"Louise, your home is lovely," announced Mary Clark, her mother-in-law. "I can see Dennis' impeccable craftsmanship everywhere and you have decorated your place beautifully." All their family members from Avinger, Texas gathered in the backyard of their new house on Iroquois Street. Louise's parents were entertaining little Flora. Her father was playfully bouncing her up and down on his lap. In turn, Flora showed how much she enjoyed it by giggling and clapping her hands.

Louise's mother scolded her father, "You're too rough with her! Now, don't you hurt her!"

"Oh hush, Anna Mae, you didn't raise our kids by yourself! I know what I'm doing!" he gloated stubbornly.

Where the coach house once stood, the men were tossing horseshoes and good-naturedly arguing among themselves about who was going to win. Dennis and Louise's nieces and nephews were cheerfully playing badminton, while the women talked and watched them play. Tammy and Henry were busy supervising their twins, who were playing on little Flora's gym set.

Deacon Reid was adopted into the family and was introduced as little Flora's uncle. He sat in a lawn chair waiting patiently for his turn to play with her. After Mrs. Caldwell's death, Louise took on the grueling task of informing Deacon Reid about the tragedy. He was heartbroken, and both he and Louise blamed themselves for not being able to protect Mrs. Caldwell. He expressed that life had cheated him once again of happiness. Dennis and Louise took on the challenge of comforting Deacon Reid.

In turn, Deacon Reid played an important part in Louise's transition from depression. He got the young couple involved in his church and there all three of them found acceptance and understanding that created an everlasting bond of friendship. In one of Deacon Reid's confessions to Louise, he mentioned how he wanted to travel. She encouraged him to do so. With no desire to travel by himself, he longed for a travelling companion. No one could take his Flora's place and he could not see the fun of travelling alone. On one of Louise's visits to the library, she found information regarding tour groups designed for senior citizens. So far, Deacon Reid had visited London, Paris, and Madrid. When he returned home, he brought back little trinkets for the young Clark family.

)0(

After Mrs. Caldwell's funeral, her children did not want anything to do with the house. Since their mother purchased it after they were adults and had moved away, it did not hold any sentimental value for them. When Dennis and Louise offered to buy it, Mrs. Caldwell's children eagerly sold the property to them. The couple used the reward money they received from the government of Mexico for the return of the missing bullion to purchase it and start a construction business. As the owner of a thriving construction company, Dennis utilized Henry as a consultant and was able to obtain many city contracts. He employed a crew of workers that included his younger brother.

Miraculously, Dennis and his crew gutted the house on Iroquois Street, changing it into a three story mansion. On the third floor were several bedrooms to house their guests. Exploiting an idea from one of the fancy hotels he helped construct, Dennis installed an elevator. His younger brother lived with them and he utilized one of the bedrooms on the third floor. The second floor housed the bedrooms for the young Clarks, their future children, and a sewing room for Louise. The first floor was similar to when Mrs. Caldwell lived there, but much more chic with a huge living room, dining room, and kitchen with a large walk in pantry. Each floor had its own unique bathroom that Deacon Reid helped to design.

For Dennis, his transition from country to city life was a dream come true. The ordeal with the bullion and Mrs. Caldwell's death taught him how gullible he was when it came to his judgment of people. He learned to trust his wife's instincts.

Dennis wanted to have a large family like the one he grew up with and he often teased Louise that he would keep her barefoot and pregnant. Louise issued a rebuttal, by saying "You wish!" Very content with her new life, Louise was pregnant again. She found happiness in raising their daughter, taking care of their home, gardening, and sewing. Little Flora was a handful, therefore, two or three children would be sufficient for her.

)0(

Dennis stopped playing horseshoes and walked over to Louise and his mother. "Ma, I love this gal," he remarked, placing his arm dotingly around Louise's waist.

Louise blushed. "And I love you back," she replied.

"I'm proud of the both of you and the new home you've made for yourselves," said Mary Clark, hugging them both. She watched them as they went off to a corner.

"Dennis, this is one of the happiest days of my life," announced Louise. I have all of my family here. I feel like a carefree child again with Mama and Daddy here. "With all that we've been through, I wouldn't want to be anyplace other than here."

"I thought I'd never here you say that," remarked Dennis.

The young Clarks compared their new life to that of their parents. Now, they also, were respective members of their new community.

978-0-595-39154-7
0-595-39154-0

Printed in the United States
56965LVS00001B/18